Beautiful

Truth's Found When Beauty's Lost

CINDY MARTINUSEN-COLOMA

THOMAS NELSON

Since 1798

NASHVILLE   DALLAS   MEXICO CITY   RIO DE JANEIRO   BEIJING

To my sister Jenny
We'll always have McCormick "Sister Power"!

Quotation on pages 92–93 is from *The Voyage of the Dawn Treader* by C. S. Lewis. © 1952 C. S. Lewis Pte. Ltd.

Published in Nashville, Tennessee by Thomas Nelson. Thomas Nelson is a trademark of Thomas Nelson, Inc.

Thomas Nelson, Inc., titles may be purchased in bulk for educational, business, fundraising, or sales promotional use. For information, please e-mail SpecialMarkets@ ThomasNelson.com.

Published in association with Books & Such Literary Agency, Janet Kobobel Grant, 52 Mission Circle, Suite 122, PMB 170, Santa Rosa, CA 95409-5370.

Library of Congress Cataloging-in-Publication Data

Martinusen-Coloma, Cindy, 1970–
  Beautiful / Cindy Martinusen-Coloma.
    p. cm.
  Summary: Much admired, beautiful, driven high school senior Ellie thinks she has her life all mapped out, but when tragedy suddenly strikes shortly after her hated grandfather's funeral, she is left to wonder what it all means.
  ISBN 978-1-59554-357-8 (softcover)
  [1. Coming of age—Fiction. 2. Burns and scalds—Fiction. 3. Disfigured persons—Fiction. 4. Interpersonal relations—Fiction. 5. Christian life—Fiction. 6. High schools—Fiction. 7. Schools—Fiction. 8. Sisters—Fiction.] I. Title.
  PZ7.M36767Be 2009
  [Fic—dc22   2009027712

Printed in the United States of America

09 10 11 12 13 RRD 6 5 4 3 2 1

Chapter 1

THE OUTSIDER
The Anonymous Blog about Life at West Redding High
October 17

Why would you ever want to be like Ellie Summerfield? Because she's popular, pretty, and—what are other P words?— how about punctual, prudish, pre-law (perhaps), perky, practical . . . All I have to say is: predictable! How does Ryan Blasin stand someone so—this is the exact word for Ellie Summerfield—*perfect*. Wanna bet she'll be back to school after her grandfather's funeral today? Just watch and see.

* * *

People were staring at Ellie as she turned the combination on her locker. She looked down and cringed. She'd meant to change from the black skirt and blouse into jeans, but the compulsion to get away had made her forget. Was that why they were staring?

"Who comes back to school after a funeral?" Vanessa opened her locker beside Ellie's.

"A person who has a calculus test sixth period and a student council meeting after school."

And a person who needs to escape her family for the rest of the day.

Ellie stared into the abyss of her locker. She really needed to reorganize. Papers stuck out from the tops of books. Her planner was missing from where it usually resided for quick reference.

"You are mistaken, Miss Summerfield. No one comes back to school after a funeral. A funeral is a free pass out of everything."

"Not everything," Ellie said and recognized how lame her defense sounded. She moved her chem book in front of her history book. She liked to keep them in the order of her classes.

"Did your sister come back to school? Of course not, and you know I never side with the sister from the dark side. Either you're more obsessive-compulsive than usual or . . . Oh, please do not tell me that you are organizing your locker—again. Take a peek into the world of the normal teen-age life."

Vanessa flung one arm toward her open locker, which overflowed with everything from papers and books to nail polish and some sort of leftover food item that Ellie didn't care to see more of. Her stomach had felt queasy off and on since her parents gave her the news about Grandfather Edward and how the cat was eating his Salisbury steak when they found him.

Vanessa shook her head. "You do know you have a problem."

"Just one?" Ellie said, closing her locker. Her phone vibrated in her purse.

Ryan: I wanted to go with you today.

"Didn't they have some post-funeral party—or dinner, whatever it's called?" Vanessa applied lip gloss as she leaned close to the mirror on the inside door of her locker, then checked her wavy blonde hair.

"Yes, and I've eaten more casseroles and store-bought desserts this week than I've had in my life."

Ellie typed on her phone:

I wished you were there. Sorry.
Ryan: Are you okay? It isn't easy burying a relative
    that you didn't like.
Ellie: I never said I didn't like him.
Ryan: You didn't have to.

Ellie slipped her phone back into her bag. She didn't want to think about her grandfather right now.

A guy across the quad pointed at her and nudged his friend. Should she wave at them?

"Am I being paranoid, or are people staring at me today?"

"You aren't being paranoid."

"What?"

"People are staring at you." Vanessa leaned back against the lockers and typed something into her phone.

"Why?" Ellie looked at the students hurrying to class.

"You were the topic of 'The Outsider' this morning."

Ellie stared at Vanessa. "What did it say?"

"Oh, just about you being perfect and stuff like that."

Ellie didn't know how to respond. "The Outsider" was the

newest popular blog, which was ironic since it was supposedly written by someone from the so-called out crowd. The unknown writer liked to comment about the in crowd, though Ellie wondered who decided the lines of in and out at their school. She'd be in no crowd if she could choose.

Vanessa brushed some lint off Ellie's skirt. "Uh, nice outfit. It also said you'd come back to school after the funeral."

Ellie's mouth dropped. "How could they know that?"

"Wouldn't it be crazy if the Outsider was Tara?" Vanessa said, motioning slightly with her head toward Tara Radcliffe, who walked toward them.

"No way. She's usually the prime target. And if anyone on earth is in the in crowd—whatever that means—she'd be the queen."

"That could all be a ruse to hide her identity."

"The Outsider writes too many mean things about her."

"True. What is she wearing?" Vanessa muttered in a voice in which Ellie heard envy as well as disdain.

Ellie's phone rumbled from inside her purse.

Ryan: We're going somewhere after school.
Ellie tapped the keys: Can't. Student council meeting.

Tara stopped in front of them. "Sorry to hear about your grandpa," she said.

Ellie looked up from her cell phone, and Vanessa frowned and squinted her eyes. Tara walked away before Ellie could respond.

"What was that about?" Ellie asked. Tara rarely talked to Ellie, and Ellie didn't care enough to wonder why. Tara rarely talked to anyone. She'd moved from New York, or so it was said. This was her first year at Redding; she'd left the big city for the small city—something about her father's company going down with many others—and she hadn't transitioned well.

"She didn't even mean that. There was not one hint of sorry in her voice."

Ellie frowned. "So everyone knows I was at my grandfather's funeral?"

"She probably knows from Ryan."

"Ryan?"

Ryan beeped in again:

Meeting canceled. You're mine after school. No
     arguing and no questions asked.

"Tara is always talking to Ryan when you aren't there. Guess she thought today was her free day. She sat at his table at lunch."

Ellie turned to watch Tara walking toward class with the confidence and movements of someone well beyond high school. Tara didn't fit here. She belonged in whatever prep school she'd come from. Did Ryan find her attractive? Of course he did. Everyone found Tara attractive even if she was a snob.

"So you think she's interested in Ryan?" Ellie knew she should feel furious, but a sudden tiredness swept over her. Her relationship with Ryan was complicated. Or maybe it was simple, and she made it complicated.

"To be retro about it . . . Duh!"

* * *

Megan carried the two glasses from the kitchen to the living room. With Ellie at school, Mom was making her remain downstairs to "be with the family" after the funeral. Their house looked like an old folks' home. She nearly tripped over a walker.

"Is that my root beer?" Uncle Henry asked.

"Yes, this is yours, and this one is for Margaret."

Margaret's hand shook as she took the glass, and Megan wondered why Uncle Henry had left Aunt Gloria for this poodle-haired, overweight lady. It had been the scandal of the assisted-living facility, apparently. At least that's what Aunt Gloria said when she and Mrs. Koleski were whispering in the kitchen. Aunt Gloria didn't need a walker yet, and she'd been so involved with the family for something like forty years that she seemed more like the blood relative than he did. Whatever was he thinking?

"I wanted a few ice cubes," Uncle Henry said without reaching for the drink.

Megan continued to hold it out to him. "You asked for no ice."

"Well, I meant maybe one or two."

Megan wanted to give him one or two, all right.

Family, isn't it great? she thought as she marched back to the kitchen. Maybe Ellie was as brilliant as everyone claimed. After all, it wasn't Ellie who was checking on elderly people because they'd been in the bathroom a long time, or taking drinks around, or returning to the kitchen for one or two ice cubes.

She caught a disapproving glance from the Leonards as she passed, and nearly said, "It's a great dress, isn't it?"

Everyone was appalled at her dress. She had sewn it herself in the week since Grandfather's death.

Mom had stared when she came downstairs. "It's very nice, but why so bright, honey? The relatives may find it disrespectful."

"They find everything about me disrespectful, so why not one more thing?"

"It was Dad's favorite color," Megan's father said, defending her. "He would have liked it, though I'm sure he wouldn't have admitted it."

And that was exactly why she'd sewn it. In homage to her grandfather—a dress of bright yellow that would shake the family up. The old man would have loved it, and she hoped he was laughing from the grave, proud of her as only Grandfather Edward ever was.

"Megan, are you going to the kitchen? Would you be a dear and bring some more of those Beanee Weenees?"

"Certainly," she said, though she couldn't remember the name of the old lady who had called out the request.

Megan just wanted a cigarette and some silence.

"That's Ellie's sister," she heard someone whisper loud enough for anyone to hear. "I don't know where Ellie is. Maybe she's too upset and needed some time."

Even with her sister gone, the family asked more questions about Ellie. Everyone loved her, thought she was beautiful and sweet and "just darling." Well, that little darling hated their grandfather; should Megan tell them that? At least Megan loved the old man—mean ole geezer that he was.

Maybe she liked him because he was the only one who liked her better than her younger sister. The only one who didn't despise her dyed black hair, her thick makeup, and her annoyance with mankind. Maybe because she was a lot like him.

Megan was the emo, the goth, the bad sister. Yet she felt she was none of those. She was simply herself. That was what none of them—not the old, decrepit family members or her high school "peers"—could understand. Drones that they were. Her sister could be their queen bee.

Megan put two ice cubes in Uncle Henry's glass—if he wished for only one, he could fish the other out himself.

"Megan, has dessert been set out yet?" Aunt Betty asked as Megan made her trek back through the crowded kitchen and living room.

"Almost. Would you like some coffee while you wait?" *Maybe I should set out a tip jar.*

"I'd like a gin and tonic."

Get in line, Aunt Betty.

"I don't think we have either—not the gin, not the tonic."

"That was a joke, dear." Aunt Betty made a *tsk*ing sound with her lips. "Coffee would be lovely. As long as it's decaf. Caffeine does funny things to me."

Megan smiled as if she understood completely and hurried to get the coffee before the stories of elderly ailments began. She'd heard all about Uncle Henry's colon, Mrs. Parks's eye surgery, and someone else's hip replacement surgery ("Did you know they hang you upside down for that? And they practically remove your whole leg!").

In the kitchen, Megan found Mom putting plastic wrap over a partially eaten casserole.

"Aunt Betty requests coffee, and someone wanted Beanee Weenees."

"Thank you so much for helping," Mom said.

"Sure," Megan said, hoping that gave her the okay to make this the last delivery. "Is this decaf?" She reached for the coffeepot.

"No, but I can make some."

Megan paused. "No, it'll be fine."

* * *

The calculus test rested on the desk in front of Ellie, but the numbers might as well have been Chinese. Calculus didn't come easy for her, but the lowest grade she'd received was a B+.

Ellie squeezed her eyes closed and then opened them again. She had come to school to forget, to jump back into her routine, to get back to normal. Maybe she'd feel better if she'd changed out of her funeral clothes. This test would be easier if she'd stop picturing her dead grandfather.

Edward Blaine Summerfield II had left the earth the Saturday before. He was found in his recliner with his head bent to the side. Beside him was a TV tray with a Hungry Man frozen dinner (Salisbury steak and mashed potatoes that the cat surely enjoyed) and an ashtray filled with ashes and cigar butts. The television was still on, tuned to Channel 9, or so Ellie guessed. Her grandfather loved PBS. He had closed his eyes a moment, and that was that.

Ellie thought of Megan during the service, wiping away smears of thick black eyeliner. Ellie wanted to be sad like that. She wanted to cry for a grandfather who had taken her on walks or introduced her to the Three Stooges. She wanted to remember his stories of war buddies and to enjoy the smell of cherry tobacco smoke. But she didn't have such memories. Grandfather Edward had hated her for as long as she could remember.

Focus, she told herself and spotted a word problem on the second page. Word problems were easier.

If geometry is the study of space, what is calculus?

A. The study of variables.

B. The study of change.

C. The study of function.

She smiled at the thought: *Life is like calculus. A study of change.* She filled in the B bubble and continued through the problems, finishing the test moments before the bell rang. Her phone rang as she walked out of Mr. Dolan's class. She'd forgotten to turn off the sound. It was Ryan's ringtone: "Electrical Storm," a U2 song she loved.

"Tired of texting?" Ellie answered.

"And I wanted to hear your voice," Ryan said with his usual underlying laughter. "The surprise was somewhat Kyle's idea, so the guys are meeting us. But you're going to love this anyway."

"Love what?" She didn't want to go on an outing, and especially not with the guys. She walked with the phone against her ear, trying to raise her usual smile as people waved and said hello. At least they weren't staring the way they'd been when she first arrived.

She reached the bench where they usually met, but Ryan wasn't there. "Where are you?"

"On my way. Turn to your right." She spotted him as she turned. Ryan leapt over a railing and down the stairs. The effortless way he moved and his easy charm were disarming, even after the day she'd had.

"Hi," she said, biting her lip. Perhaps it was the day's events, but she felt a sudden longing for him to hold her tightly against him and tell her that everything would be okay.

Six months had passed since they started going out, and Ellie still wasn't sure why they were together. They were different in so many ways, though most everyone at school thought they made the perfect couple. She guessed that Tara wasn't one of them.

Ryan kissed her then and held her chin—which he said he adored. His initial carefree expression changed to concern. "How was the funeral? You okay?"

"Fine. It was fine. I'm fine. But listen, whatever happens, whatever kind of resistance you encounter, do not forget what I'm about to tell you."

"It will be seared into my memory." He looked at her intently, making her smile.

"I absolutely and positively do not want organ music at my funeral."

"Great," he said and kissed her chin.

Vanessa came up behind them. "Great? She's talking about her funeral, and you say great?"

"It's great that she's planning to have me still around when she dies—as an old and wise woman, of course."

That caught Ellie off guard. She'd meant it more as a joke. "I didn't mean to imply that, or presume—it was just, you know . . ."

Ryan took her book bag from her arm. "Don't start analyzing, Els. It's okay. I'm not taking it as a marriage proposal. That'll be my job anyway." He smiled like the Cheshire cat and put his arm over her shoulder. "Don't analyze that, either. Let's just get out of here. Wanna come, Vanessa?"

"Where?" Vanessa walked beside Ellie, texting on her phone.

"I can't tell you, but you'll be gone at least an hour and a half, and you'll be glad you came. It's a once-in-several-decades opportunity."

"What could that be, an eclipse?" Vanessa looked up at the sky, searching for the sun.

Ryan laughed. "No, it is not an eclipse."

"I can't. I start work at my mother's sweat factory today."

"Her what?" Ellie asked. "I thought your mom owned a consulting business."

Vanessa sighed as if her life was the hardest on the planet. "She does. And since Dad was laid off and Mom brings home the moola, guess who has to help in the office or not have any spending money?"

"Um, your dad?" Ryan said with a smile.

Vanessa gave him an annoyed look. "I wish. He's even busier now looking for a job than he was actually having one. So, yes, I'm glad it's sort of in vogue to be poor. I'm always fashionably ahead of the times. If you need me, look for me buried beneath papers to file or manning the phone lines of Caroline Von's IT Consulting."

Ryan's phone rang, and he turned away from Ellie to talk without her hearing. "It's a surprise, remember."

Vanessa slid her arm through Ellie's and smiled as a text beeped on Ellie's phone.

12

Beautiful

Vanessa: Don't break up with Ryan before home-
    coming. I might go with Drew, and I want us to
    go together.

Ellie stopped. "What are you talking about?"

Vanessa shook her head, glancing at Ryan. "We'll talk about it later. But sometimes I know you better than you know you."

"Not this time," Ellie said as they reached the parking lot. Then she smiled at Vanessa. "Enjoy the factory."

"Gee, thanks."

Ryan ended the call and took Ellie's hand. "Everything okay?" he asked.

She nodded, thinking about Vanessa's text. Sometimes, often actually, Ellie did have her doubts. Maybe it would be better for them to break up now instead of being committed to something that couldn't last forever. But as Ryan put his arm around her, Ellie knew it wouldn't be today or this week. Whether they were right for each other or not, Ryan was the first person to make her almost believe in love.

Chapter 2

THE OUTSIDER

The Anonymous Blog about Life at West Redding High

October 17

This was never supposed to be a daily blog, let alone a twice-in-one-day blog, but with the high volume of comments, I'll comment back. Why not? It's not like any of you think I have anything better to do. But then, you don't know who I am, do you?

We had 40 comments about Ellie Summerfield coming back to school after her grandfather's funeral. What did I say? Predictable. Some geek sent live streaming video from his cell phone—<u>click here</u> to view. My next blog will be about the Geek Revolution—you just gotta admire those geeks.

I will note that Ellie's sister, Megan, didn't return to school, but why write about her, since she's one of the invisibles like 80 percent of the high school population?

Aristotle said, "The aim of art is to represent not the outward appearance of things, but their inward significance." What kind of art would be used to represent the inward significance of Ellie Summerfield and others like her? Stick figures? Play-Doh sculptures? That was mean, I know, but seriously . . .

* * *

R yan opened the door to his '68 Mustang. Ellie's phone beeped a reminder.

"I forgot to check about the student council meeting—"

Ryan motioned for her to get in. "They didn't think you'd be there, so they canceled it."

The inside of the car had a sultry warmth, making her instantly sleepy. Ryan closed her door, then rounded the front, his hand as always nearly skimming the waxed, charcoal-colored hood. Just one of his endearing unconscious quirks.

"They could've had the meeting without me," Ellie said as Ryan sat behind the wheel.

He turned and touched her chin. "I doubt that. You'd better train an apprentice before you graduate. I don't think this school will know how to operate once you're gone."

The engine roared to life. Ellie loved the sound of it. Ryan's father had bought it during college, and the two of them had restored it before Ryan was handed the keys. It got terrible gas mileage, but despite her belief in renewable resources, caring for the planet, and the school campaign she organized about ways to conserve energy, Ellie couldn't deny a love for this classic, gas-guzzling, beautiful beast. Plus, his family owned a hybrid, so that had to balance out their carbon footprint.

"I don't really want to be around the guys. Couldn't we just go to Cocobeans?" Ellie leaned back in the seat and felt the rumble of the engine and the beat of John Mellencamp. Ryan had given her a whole history of the older rocker, his years as John Cougar and how he'd become an American icon, though Ellie had never heard of him before. She closed her eyes and wished they could just sit right here for a few minutes with the engine and the music and the warmth inside the car. It even smelled good—a subtle mix of Ryan's cologne with vinyl cleaner, perhaps.

Ryan rested his elbow on the seat and touched just one strand of her hair. The touch sent chills down the back of her neck.

"You want to go to Cocobeans because you don't want to go home, yet you don't want too much quiet, but you don't want to hang out with people you know, either—except for me."

She gave him a sideways glance as he put the car in reverse and backed out. How did he get her so perfectly at times? The thing was, she would've liked to go somewhere right now, with or without him. If her Karmann Ghia hadn't broken down again, she'd take it out for a long drive, maybe even to the coast and then north along the Pacific Highway to Oregon, Washington, and Canada. A road trip sounded perfect, if only she didn't have classes and committees and her senior project.

"I'm avoiding my house. It's just full of relatives and—"

"Uh-huh. Deny all you want. But this time, I'm kidnapping you. We have to do this." Before she could protest, he interrupted. "Hey, let me see the bracelet." He slowed down at a stoplight and leaned forward.

Ellie had nearly forgotten it and held up her wrist for him to see the antique gold woven together and attached with a dainty clasp.

"It's beautiful, and it actually fits your wrist. So you think your grandfather is turning over in his grave?"

"Most likely," she said, looking at the etching in the gold. Her father had presented it to her earlier that morning, saying, "Now you have something of your grandmother's."

As a young girl, Ellie had picked out this very bracelet from her grandmother's jewelry box. Her grandfather had caught her and had slapped her hands, each one of them, and threatened to slap her face if he ever found her in that room again. Her mother and father had been furious. It was the last time they all went to visit him. Ellie would see Grandpa Edward at various holidays here and there when a temporary treaty was made . . . until he did something else that upset her generally amiable parents.

"I bet your grandmother would love knowing you have it, Els. Your grandfather was messed up, that's all."

That's all. And for Ryan such things were folded up and put away just like that. Ellie wished she could let go of things as easily. To not overthink and analyze everything. Especially now. With her grandfather dead, Ellie would never know why he disliked her so. Not even her parents had the answer.

She leaned back against the seat. The song about little pink houses came on, and Ellie wished she could sink deep inside the seat and into the music. It would be safe there, she thought.

* * *

Megan was stretched out on her bed, listening to an alternative band and reading their bios on her laptop, when the guilt got to her.

"How harmful could caffeine be?" she said aloud, picturing Aunt Betty doubled over in pain or racing around the house like an old woman on speed.

She went downstairs, back to the noise of old voices telling old stories.

"I wondered where you went," Aunt Betty called when she saw Megan. "I'd like another cup of coffee. You really should be helping your mother, dear."

Megan took the cup and said in a sickly sweet voice, "More decaf, Aunt Betty?"

"Of course, dear." Aunt Betty shook her head and said to someone beside her, "I think my memory is better than hers."

"Coming right up, then."

A text beeped on her phone as she carried the cup of coffee.

James: Are you still in the yellow dress?
Megan: I'm wearing it all day as my tribute.

She looked at her hand. She'd worn her grandmother's antique ring as a tribute as well. Grandfather Edward had specifically asked Megan to have it—and told her that he didn't want that silly daughter-in-law to get her paws on it. Her father had given Ellie their grandmother's bracelet to make up for the fact that Grandfather Edward hadn't set aside anything for her.

James: You just like stirring up trouble. But you in
        yellow and in a dress, I'm dying to see.
Megan: And I look quite good in it too.

She poured another cup of "decaf" for Aunt Betty. Grandfather Edward would've laughed about this one. He really would have loved it if the caffeine actually did make Aunt Betty feel "funny."

Megan saw a car pull into the driveway and recognized several ladies from church. Would this day ever end?

James: Meet me tonight at Tonya's.

He was trouble, she could tell already. But a little trouble might be nice about now.

Megan: I'm not wearing the dress.
James: I'll take you in any color you want.

Trouble, here I come.

* * *

They stood in a single line along the edge of the bluff. No one spoke for a moment as Ellie, Ryan, Tank, Kevin, and Bly stared down at what had once been an arm of Lake Shasta. Ellie had never seen anything like it. The lake was gone. Only a wide, shallow river remained. If not for the I-5 bridge and signs that said *Lakehead*, she wouldn't have believed this.

Bly broke the silence. "This is the lowest the lake has been in sixteen years. A bunch of old bridges and roads are visible that were under the water since the dam was built in 1945. There's even an old tunnel and a complete metal bridge out in the center of the lake."

"Where?" Tank asked.

"Just around the corner." Bly wiped his forehead as he always did when he gave one of his lengthy explanations.

Ellie loved Ryan and his friends for the way they took a scrawny childhood friend and kept him near. Sure, they loved it when he drank and they asked him questions of philosophy or to recite some poetry, which wasn't really noble. But they cared for him. He was their small Irish bard. And they protected him in a way that reminded her more of a parental guardianship than the usual guy bond.

"Good research, Bly," Kevin said, smacking him on the back and making him lose his balance. Kevin grabbed his shirt. "Whoa, there, little fella."

Ellie could just imagine Bly tumbling down the hillside into the stream below.

"My family camped up this arm of the lake a few years ago," Ryan said, taking Ellie's hand. "It's got to be down over a hundred feet."

"A hundred and fifty, and expected to drop even more unless we get rain," Bly called as he hurried by.

The guys raced ahead down an old stairway toward the shallow river that wound along the bottom of the canyon.

"So this is what it looked like before the dam was built," Ellie said, amazed by the surreal knowledge that under normal conditions they'd be going underwater right now.

"Look what I found," Bly yelled, holding up a square glass bottle. "I think it's an antique. Maybe an old cowboy drank it."

"Yeah, a cowboy who liked Jack Daniels."

"Jack Daniels?" Bly looked at the bottle again in disappointment.

The steps descended sharply, narrowing to nearly straight

down. Ryan held Ellie's hand tightly. She'd traded her black heels for an old pair of her flip-flops Ryan had found nearly forgotten in the corner of his trunk, left there after one of their summer outings. The guys had already scattered in their exploration.

"We'd be underneath hundreds of gallons of water by this point," Ryan said, pointing to the waterline above them.

"Hey, over here!" one of the guys called from around the bend.

"Come on, Els." Ryan tugged at her hand.

"Go ahead. I'll be there soon."

He gave her a quick exploratory look, then nodded and hurried off like a kid running toward a carnival.

Ellie stepped carefully along the rocks. She wished she were in jeans and a sweatshirt, but she had to admit Ryan had brought her to a great place. She slid on her butt, careful not to catch her skirt as she went down a drop of slick rock. The earth all around held a red hue, and along the edges of the stream, pools of water were bloodred from the mineral deposits.

"It looks like we're on Mars," she said, though no one was near enough to hear. Only the thick pines that crowded together on the top half of the surrounding mountains reminded her that she was on earth. The line between the two was sudden where the waterline should be, creating a sharp contrast between this former underwater world and the earth world above it.

The bracelet slid low on her wrist. Her grandfather was dead. The funeral was over. Ellie had to get back to her old self again. Organized, focused, dependable. Remembering what needed to be done and doing it. Homecoming and then winter formal were coming. She'd stepped out of being the chair so that she could focus on the food drive and actually enjoy the dance. Her gold dress was already on hold, and it was stunning and eye-catching, something she didn't usually wear. But it was senior year, so why not step out further—or so she'd thought on the day she'd picked it out. Today it didn't appeal to her. She wondered if she and Ryan would even be together in the months ahead.

She reached the wide but shallow river that ran along the bottom of the canyon. Downstream, the green rafters of the massive highway bridge towered above the rippling water.

"We're at the bottom of the lake," Kevin yelled, then acted as if he were swimming. "Where did all that water go?"

"Probably being drained down to Southern California and all those city dwellers," Tank said in disgust.

"We're in the second year of a drought," Bly relayed.

The guys continued to yell back and forth as Ellie watched a flock of Canada honkers fly loudly overhead in their V formation.

"The fish must be crowded together closer to the dam. It'd be easy fishing," Kevin said.

"Let's go fishing," Tank called.

"I need my pole."

"Els, you've got to come see this," Ryan called, jumping over rocks to reach her.

She walked carefully along the rocks. One step sank her foot down into the mud. Around the bend where the river deepened and looked more like the lake, she reached Ryan. Rising from the muddy blue water were steel girders with both ends unattached. It looked like a bridge sitting alone like an island, with no road connecting either side.

"What is it?" she asked in amazement, grabbing Ryan's hand as he started to slide while coming up the muddy slope.

"It's the old railroad bridge," he said.

"Hey, look over there." Bly pointed farther down and near another bend. "I think that's Tunnel No. 7."

"This is incredible," Ellie said. She'd grown up water-skiing, wakeboarding, and boating all over this lake. And all that time there were bridges, old roads, a town, railroad trestles, and tunnels beneath the surface, forgotten and encased in time and water.

"The town of Kennett was located a few miles south," Bly said in his tour-guide voice.

"Can you see the town now?" Ellie asked, wondering how it could have survived sixty years underwater.

"No, but I heard you can see part of a tower used in the construction of Shasta Dam and a few buildings on the hills surrounding Kennett. Kennett wasn't some little no-name town. It was pretty busy. It had a copper-smelting factory. But I think it was a pretty rough place. There were dozens of saloons, and it was notorious for its fights."

"Sounds like my kind of town," Kevin said with a wide grin.

Ryan held Ellie's hand tightly as they stared across the water at the bridge. "Just imagine Model T Fords driving up and down this canyon, or even further back to stagecoaches and wagon trains."

Ellie unconsciously touched her wrist and knew something was wrong. She looked down. "Where's my bracelet?" she said to herself, turning her arm this way and that.

Ryan grabbed her wrist, then looked down at the red earth. "You had it in the car. Maybe it fell off in there?"

"No, I had it on while we were walking. I noticed it, was thinking about it."

"We'll find it, then. Hey, guys, Els lost her bracelet."

The guys immediately jumped into action.

"Was it valuable?" Kevin asked with his eyes toward the ground.

She nodded, unable to speak.

"It's very valuable," Ryan said in earnest.

The guys looked for a time, running up and down the slope, mostly in places Ellie hadn't been. She and Ryan carefully retraced her steps as best they could remember. Soon the others lost interest, and it was just her and Ryan going over and over her steps, searching for a glint of gold among the rocks.

"It'll be dark soon," Ellie said after a while as the last of the sun fell behind the mountains.

"My dad's neighbor has a metal detector." Ryan was already punching numbers into his cell phone. "We might find a fortune of stuff out here while we're at it."

She knew he was trying to lighten the mood. But a panic fluttered in her stomach. It was the first heirloom she'd been given, from a grandmother she wished she had known. Her grandfather's death allowed it to be hers. And now so quickly, she'd lost it? This meant something. Something bad.

Ellie wasn't superstitious, not usually. Her faith was in God—she truly believed that God loved her, and she tried to love Him back. She lived with the secure sense that He would take care of her life in the ways she could not. She knew losing a bracelet didn't signify anything other than a loose clasp.

So why was it having this effect on her entire body? Her stomach hurt, and her hands were shaking so badly that Ryan grabbed hold of them and pressed his large hands around them while he talked on the phone, detailing what they needed and asking if that could happen tonight.

"My dad's neighbor isn't home now, and Dad's leaving early for a business trip to Sacramento. But we're set for Saturday. He said he'd rent another metal detector if he needs to. So don't worry, 'k, Els?"

She nodded and couldn't respond for a moment, feeling the tears well up in her eyes. "I should go home."

"Are you okay?"

"It's been a long day," she said as he put his arm around her waist.

"Hey," he called to Bly. Tank and Kevin had run ahead to check out Tunnel No. 7. "We're going. We'll catch up tomorrow."

Bly nodded, and Ellie tried to wave good-bye, but the weight of loss was heavy upon her. Heavier than the funeral. What kind of person felt more sorrow over a lost bracelet than over the death of a grandfather? Grandfather Edward was gone, and there'd never be reconciliation; there'd never be peace in the memory of him. And now it was as if he'd won again. The bracelet was gone.

"We're going to get it back. I promise," Ryan said, and for a moment she almost believed him.

* * *

They drove back in a comfortable silence with the music loud and soothing at her back. Ellie stared out the window, trying to rid herself of the sick feeling. And somehow the drive through the mountains and down into the valley did relax her, until they pulled in front of the small gray-and-white two-story house with the driveway still packed with cars. For a moment she saw it as a stranger might, just another average house with a lawn that was due for a mowing and shrubs that needed reshaping, but otherwise cute and pretty for the somewhat common neighborhood.

"You know," Ryan said as she turned to him, "there are two times you're the most beautiful."

She couldn't help but smile at the way he said this. "When are those?"

"When you get all dreamy and deep in thought—like just then, when you were staring out the window. Right now, with that doubtful look on your face, that's another story. Doubtful—not your best look."

Ellie gave him a little punch to his arm, and he gave an exaggerated wince.

"And the other time," he said, laughing, "is exactly right now, when you're smiling. That smile could stop a guy's heart."

He reached to turn off the ignition, but Ellie stopped him with a hand on his arm.

"Don't come in. I'm going to bed as soon as possible." She leaned her head back against the headrest. The seats were warm, and a light thump beat through her back from the stereo's bass. She breathed in deeply and wished to stay there, safe and warm, with the faint scent of Ryan's cologne. The windows were up, their little space encapsulated. He patted his shoulder, and she leaned her head to rest there, a gesture that was familiar and still as comforting as the first time she'd leaned her head against him during their first movie date.

"It's okay. It'll be okay."

And she wondered what he meant by that. Was he talking about the loss of her bracelet or life in general?

He motioned toward her house. Mom was peering out into the darkness and gave a wave for her to come inside.

"I'm guessing I have lots of old relatives who missed me this afternoon."

"I don't mind coming in," he said.

"Thanks. I just want to say hello and then get to my room—or rather, Megan's room. My room continues to be overrun with old people. I'll need to air out flowery perfume for the next week."

"By the way, we are going out tomorrow night."

Ellie smiled. "Is this the promised date?"

"It is. It's the special night."

Her smile wavered a moment. "*The* special night?"

Before he could respond, Mom flicked the porch light on and off.

"We'll stop by Mitch's dad's house later. We don't have to stay long, but Mitch would be hurt if I didn't bring you by, when he's only down for the weekend."

Stopping by a party that would have all the usual high-school party elements sounded as appealing as a game night with her parents and their church friends. But "the special night" held its own stress. What exactly did Ryan expect on such a night? He knew where she stood, yet he also bragged about his ability to charm the coat off a homeless man in winter—which he actually had done for a fund-raiser scavenger hunt the previous winter. He'd given a better coat back to the man—goose down and with a hood—and the entire act became a classic story among the staff at the mission.

Tank said Ryan only volunteered in order to get in Ellie's pants, and that no girl was worth charity work. But Tank's theory was proven false in the six celibate months of their dating.

"You do remember that I was on the committee of SADD? Parties don't usually like to see me coming."

"It'll be short, just a few minutes there."

They kissed good-bye, and Ellie thought how entwined their lives were now. They planned the weekends together; they kissed good-bye; he had expected to come to the funeral, and she would've had him there if the funeral were for anyone other than her grandfather.

Ellie got out of the car and closed the door. She bent to wave once more, and Ryan motioned her to his window.

"Hey," he said, "I'm going to say this now because you've had a bad day with the funeral and I want you to know, but it's not for you to stress over. Just accept it and move on from there."

"Uh, okay."

"I'm going to say this and leave so you don't have to respond."

She waited.

"I love you."

She stared at him. He really meant it, his first "I love you" to anyone he'd ever dated.

Ryan waved then, with a sad smile, and drove away before she could respond.

* * *

"Sweetie, there are so many people who want to say hello to you. You've been gone so long." Mom had that tone in her voice—cheerful disapproval. "The ladies from the church brought dinner."

She ushered Ellie inside to the waiting relatives and family friends who sat around on the couches and folding chairs with food-laden paper plates in their laps.

Ryan had just said he loved her.

An elderly man who looked familiar called to her from the love seat by the cold fireplace. "There you are, Elspeth."

The woman next to him said, "We brought photographs of our trip to Texas. And Jasper brought those old war photos of your grandfather as well."

Ellie and Ryan used the *love* word at times. *Love ya. That's what I love about you. Love me too. I just love how you . . .* But they hadn't said the full-blown, straight-out words yet.

"I have some stories to tell you about your grandfather," said a lady who had come up beside her.

Ellie wondered where Megan was.

Should she send Ryan a text in response? What would she say? Could she text *I love you back*? Make a joke, be serious—what should she do?

"Ellie, show Aunt Tina the bracelet. She doesn't remember

it. I can't believe you don't remember it." Mom turned to Dad's younger sister.

Mom and Aunt Tina looked at her, waiting. The elderly couple waited. The older woman too.

"I . . ." she said, raising her hand, pausing to find the right words. "I left it in Ryan's car."

"Honey, that's a family heirloom." Cheerful disapproval again, with a touch more disapproval.

"I know. I'll get it tomorrow."

"Okay," Mom said with disappointment. "I'll show you later, Tee."

"Jane, I'm stealing your daughter away. Come here, young lady," the older woman said to Mom.

Mrs. Leonard—Ellie suddenly remembered that was her name—held up a large stack of photographs.

So much for going to bed.

It seemed as if from the moment Grandfather died until now that a free pass had been handed to all of their family and friends, allowing everyone to talk about his life and to make their assumptions. They told stories about someone who sounded nothing like the angry man Ellie had known. His sisters talked about how he'd been as a kid and teenager. How close they'd all been. Then there were the speculations about why he'd become so mean. There were revelations of grudges and entire branches of the family tree that she'd never heard of or known about, like Grandfather's older brother who told Mom when she called with the news of his death, "I stopped thinking I had a brother many years ago. He wasn't a nice man. And I won't be coming to the funeral."

"You're a lot like your grandfather, you know?" Mrs. Leonard said.

Then she touched Ellie's arm, and Ellie realized that she'd said it to *her*, not to Megan, who was walking by.

"What?" Ellie asked and saw the look of disgust on her sister's face.

"You are a lot like your grandfather. When he was young, of course. He was quite the young man. Had such a passion for life, so very smart like you, able to do anything he put his mind to."

"We had nothing in common," Ellie said as politely as she could.

She sat through the stories and the photographs, acting interested and positive about it all. Her elderly relatives thought of her as confident and strong; most adults did. She supposed that was her fault for acting the part. All evening Ellie heard, either directly or indirectly, how much she had going for her, what a beautiful young woman she had become, how proud they all were of her.

Did you see the younger daughter—yes, she is younger, by only eleven months or something. She'll do something great with her life, you can just tell.

The comparisons inevitably came out. For a reason known only to her parents, they had put Megan and Ellie into kindergarten at the same time. That Ellie excelled at everything in school further aggravated the differences between the sisters. The closeness they'd had as little girls broke down step-by-step as the years passed, as teachers and classmates compared and commented. People often thought they were twins, with very different personalities, looks, and achievements. One was good. The other was bad.

Ellie didn't understand why Megan didn't try to make any of it better. She barely passed her classes; she dressed in whatever way would cause unrest. Ellie expected the piercings to begin as soon as Megan turned eighteen. She'd already gotten two tattoos that Mom and Dad didn't know about.

Ellie's stomach rumbled loudly, and the sudden need for food pulsed through her. "Excuse me, Mrs. Leonard, while I grab a snack. It's been a long day."

The dining room looked like a church potluck. Ellie picked up a paper plate and silverware rolled up in a napkin.

"I bet you haven't eaten." Dad walked along the opposite side of the food table.

"Guess I'll make up for it now. I bet you haven't eaten all day either."

His confession came with a grin.

"Oh, there she is," a voice said, followed by another voice echoing. Aunt Betty and Aunt Molly surrounded her as several of her cold prawns slid off the tiny plate and landed in a red Jell-O salad.

"Your parents said that you went back to school," Aunt Betty said, as usual being the official sister spokesperson.

"I had a calculus test."

"Well, you should be with family. Your mother probably needed you, and of course—" She nodded toward Ellie's dad, who was making a quick exit. "He just lost his father, and you should be here. That was very unlike you, Elspeth. Your sister did help a little, when she'd come out of her room." Aunt

Betty raised her voice as she spotted Megan getting her phone charger with a brownie in hand.

"You're welcome," Megan said.

"And why would you wear that dress today?" Aunt Betty asked, crossing her arms at her chest.

Megan shook her head and walked away.

Ellie still couldn't believe that Megan had sewn the dress in just one week. Ellie couldn't sew a button back on a shirt. The dress was canary yellow—completely inappropriate for a funeral, according to Aunt Betty. Aunt Molly's nod reminded Ellie of a bobblehead.

"Grandfather loved yellow," Ellie said, which, now that she thought of it, didn't seem a likely Grandpa characteristic. If things had been different, she would've worn a yellow dress in his honor as well.

"It doesn't matter. That isn't something that should be worn on such a day . . ."

And off they went, talking about Megan and praising Ellie for all the good that she'd done at school and church and in the community. It made even Ellie sick to hear it.

"Be right back," she said, opening the back door.

She closed the door behind her, and the noise of the house turned off like a light switch and the nighttime peace flipped on. "I thought this would be over," she exclaimed under her breath. The western sky held a final line of dark purple, and leaves littered the patio with yellow and red from the liquid amber and cottonwood trees.

"It could last for days," a voice said. A guy was sitting off to the side of the patio.

"Sorry. I didn't know anyone was out here."

Ellie looked toward the voice and recognized Will Stefanos, a classmate and neighbor. They'd been friends when they were little. There were photographs of him at summer barbecues, and Ellie had made forts with him in grade school. She lingered at the door, unwilling to return to the relatives inside, though she realized she'd left her plate of food on the buffet table.

"Sorry, but this is my spot. You could go to your room."

Ellie smiled. "My aunts are staying in my room. You could go home."

"Ouch."

"I didn't mean it that way. Just that it is a few doors away, after all."

"Yeah, I'm supposed to talk to you though."

"Talk to me?"

"You know, comfort you and Megan, tell you everything is going to be okay. My mother's commission. She sent me with a plate of brownies."

"Ah, I see. The 'go make sure everything's all right with little Ellie Summerfield' commission."

"Exactly. As well as the reminders of how you and I were best friends in preschool and I used to draw you pictures every day."

"You did?" Then Ellie remembered. "Oh yeah. They included a lot of weird little monsters, if I remember correctly."

"Aliens."

"Oh, is that what they were?"

"Yes, all my early works included aliens."

"You aren't doing a very good job of comforting us."

"I didn't see you, so I slipped out here a minute." He raised his hand, and she saw that it held a cigarette. The gray smoke took a short trail and disappeared against the darker night sky.

"Where did you go?" Ellie asked suddenly, walking over to sit in a chair closer to him.

"When?"

"When you moved in fourth grade, but you didn't move, 'cause your parents were still here."

"Brazil. To be with my grandfather, actually."

The sliding glass door opened, letting out the noise of people talking, and farther off some music from the forties played.

Ellie cringed and whispered, "Don't say anything. Maybe they won't see me."

But it was Megan. "Hey, some relatives that we're supposed to care about are leaving, and you're supposed to come say good-bye."

"Which relatives?"

"I don't know—George and Kathy something, or Bob and Kathy—I can't remember." She noticed Will then. "Hey."

He nodded in her direction, taking a drag from his cigarette. "You going tonight?"

Megan glanced at Ellie. "I think so."

"See you then."

Megan disappeared back inside the house, shutting off the sound and restoring the peace of the night.

"You and my sister are friends?"

"Yeah," he said. "Why is that weird?"

"I didn't know she had friends."

"What do you know about her?"

"That she's unhappy."

"Unhappy here, maybe."

"What does that mean?"

"Whatever you want it to mean."

Will was good-looking in a way, she realized. Sort of funky or something. Black pants and white T-shirt. Who wore a T-shirt to a funeral dinner? Perfect for someone who hung out with a girl who sewed a funky yellow dress for a funeral. His black hair was thick and cut short. She'd seen him at the mall, wearing a packer hat that looked like something from a classic movie.

"Are you and my sister . . ."

"Are we . . . what?"

Ellie shook her head and suddenly hated her black skirt and blouse. She felt like a librarian in the presence of a rock musician. "Are you going out?"

"No. Do you know anything about your sister?"

"Not really."

He stared at her then, a long, probing stare that made her want to leave and reminded her that Bob or George and Kathy were waiting for her to say good-bye.

"Maybe you should change that. I mean, you are . . ." His voice drifted off.

"I'm what?"

He looked away and took a drag, blowing the smoke out over his shoulder.

"You're Ellie Summerfield."

"What's that supposed to mean?"

He glanced at her and laughed slightly. "Don't you have some departing guests waiting for you?"

"Tell me first what that's supposed to mean. That I'm Ellie Summerfield."

"No one tells you, huh?"

"What? Just state your little observation. What do people say about me? That I'm an overachiever, a snob . . ."

"No." He laughed again. "That you can do anything. You'll help anyone. You'd give your last dollar and not expect anything back. That you're going to do great things in the world."

Was he being sarcastic? She couldn't tell. And suddenly she didn't want to know.

"I'll see you around," she said and went inside.

Mom spotted her. "You missed saying good-bye to Bob and Nancy. They waited for you. Didn't Megan tell you?"

"I don't even know who they are," she said.

"Nancy was my best friend when I was a kid."

"I was talking to someone."

"Oh, okay. Did you call Ryan to see if he has your bracelet?"

Someone called for Mom from the kitchen, and Ellie took the chance to duck into the half bathroom that was next to the laundry room. Without turning on the light, she locked the door, closed the toilet lid, and sat down. She could stay here until it was quiet.

* * *

Megan shook her head. Guys. Did they ever think with their brains?

Will liked to act the part of original Bohemian with his baggy slacks, long drags on a cigarette, and writeresque sweaters—or even better, his blazer over a T-shirt. It worked for him. The girls liked it. It might have worked for her if she hadn't known Will since they were children. Megan couldn't look at him without picturing the little boy who ate paste in kindergarten.

So now Will had one minute alone with Miss USA and he was all into her. Truth was, Will had had a thing for Ellie since they were kids. Off and on, he'd ask about who she was dating or what she was doing. One time Megan told him to go ask her himself. When Ellie started dating Ryan, he'd actually sounded angry. "Why would she date Ryan Blasin? What's wrong with her? She's becoming less and less original."

Megan wondered when Ellie had ever been original, but she kept that to herself.

She closed her bedroom door with satisfaction. Her duties as bereaved granddaughter were officially over, in her opinion. She'd helped all afternoon and into the night. Now it was music and talking with friends online and then going out later on, which included seeing James. She decided to shower and change into something else.

The funeral program for Grandfather Edward caught her eye. Suddenly she wondered if he'd felt any pain.

The last time she'd seen her grandfather was over the summer. She stayed a few days with him when her parents went away for their anniversary. She'd cleaned his house, which sorely needed it; then they watched Clint Eastwood movies and smoked in the living room side by side. Grandfather didn't care if she drank or went out after he went to sleep.

Megan had planned to visit him more, promised it, even. But the weeks passed so quickly. In a month she'd be eighteen. For this one month, she and Ellie were both seventeen. Ellie was the accident that intruded into Megan's life, making her a big sister after less than a year of life.

James had sent her several texts that she'd ignored until now. He liked her, she knew it. And she liked him, though he didn't know. Megan wasn't sure she wanted to get involved with another musician. They didn't listen or play well with others. It was all about them. But James did seem different. He certainly could play the guitar. And he'd never be attracted to someone like her sister. That was a plus.

* * *

Ellie didn't last an hour without her cell phone or computer in the bathroom. If she'd had those, she could've stayed there all night. But at least most people were gone when she crept out and upstairs to Megan's room.

She lay on the blow-up mattress on her sister's floor, trying to decide whether to address Ryan's "I love you" over text or not, when her sister hopped up from bed, fully dressed—back in her usual black—and walked out the bedroom door with the stealth of a spy.

There was no sound of her departure, no outside doors opening or closing, but Ellie knew Megan was gone. She lay there in the dark, phone in hand. Who was her sister anyway?

The walls of Megan's room had been stripped of posters and pictures. She'd painted it gray with red arrows pointing around the room to one wall and then down to a small dot in the center. In a few months, she would paint the whole thing over with a new design. Her walls were her palette, Ellie supposed.

Ellie liked her room better, decorated in a sort of French baroque mixed with funky lanterns and strings of white lights. Aunt Beatrice had pursed her lips upon entry.

Ryan: Night Els. Sorry about your bracelet. I'll find it.

If he wasn't going to bring it up, she wouldn't either, though it surely weighed heavily on him. He had told her that he'd never say those words unless he was completely serious and completely in love.

She typed: Thanks for the lake trip. It was incredible, except for the bracelet thing.
Then she cringed as she wrote: Night. Love ya.

After an hour of tossing and turning, Ellie rose and slipped a sweater over her shoulders. Opening Megan's bedroom window, she pushed the screen open on its hinge and climbed out. It was as easy as in her own room. She climbed up the roof to the spot above the dormer window of her bedroom.

She hadn't been out here in a year or so. There was a haze in the air around the streetlights down the road, and the night smelled of burning leaves and autumn.

Ellie thought of God then, as she usually did when sitting on the roof. The first time she'd come out here, she'd been praying about something and had read a verse about someone climbing a watchtower and waiting for God's answer. This was her watchtower.

Now she wondered at the distance she felt between herself and God. When had that happened? He felt farther than the dimmest stars.

No matter how many people said she was amazing, Ellie never felt she'd reached what she was supposed to reach, or overcome some dark force that chased at her heels.

For years Ellie had pushed down her grandfather's words. She could take them out today, unfold them like a worn-out letter she'd read and hidden too many times. He was dead now. He could never recant. He could never explain why he had seemed to hate her so deeply.

Mittens came pattering lightly up the roof, distracting her thoughts with his soft meow.

"How's my old kitty? I bet you hate all these people in your house. But you love me, don't you?"

He purred loudly and rolled to his side as she petted him.

Ellie could see Will's house from this part of the roof. He was gone to wherever it was Megan had left for. She hadn't invited Ellie to come along, of course. Ellie usually figured Megan was hanging out with people she shouldn't be hanging out with. Was Will one of them? And why was she suddenly feeling left out?

A lonely chill crept over her, and she pulled her sweater closer around her shoulders. Her baggy pajama bottoms were thin, and she felt goose bumps rise on her calves and thighs.

Something else was nagging at her. A lot of somethings. About Ryan. And about her grandfather. And something about herself as well.

* * *

Ellie never heard her sister come home. When her cell phone buzzed at 6:00 a.m., she heard Megan groan and rolled over to see her sister hide her head under the pillow. Ellie didn't want to get up, but she dragged herself out, determined not to wait another day to get back to normal.

When she came in sweaty and out of breath after her morning run, Dad was pouring himself a cup of coffee.

"Well, if it isn't Rosy Cheeks."

Which meant her face was beet red like it always got when she ran. But at least Dad sounded like himself again. Maybe now that the funeral was over they'd all get back to normal.

Megan was up, too, sitting on a bar stool, with her black hair sticking up and dark circles under her eyes. "Why not add the Olympics to your goals for world domination?"

"Funny."

"You aren't normal, you do realize that? I should be sleeping, but someone gets up before dawn on a Saturday morning. There's something seriously wrong with that."

"Just because I have goals and dreams . . ." Ellie began, but Megan was shuffling toward the stairs with her coffee cup in hand. She cursed under her breath, and for a moment Ellie wanted to call, "Mom, Megan said a bad word!" as if they were ten and eleven again.

For some reason this thought made her forgive Megan. Whatever her sister had been going through for the past, well, forever, she had to come out of it sometime. Mom assured her it might take till they both left for college—different colleges, preferably.

"Ellie, your mom and I need to talk to you soon," Dad said as he poked his head out of the refrigerator, where he was digging around.

"What about?"

"Your career plans. Your mother is concerned."

Ellie made a face. "Where are Mom and the aunts?"

"Early-bird prices at Macy's."

"I'll tell Mom that it's what God wants me to do. How can she argue with that?"

He turned around. "Is that what you think?"

She shrugged. It had been a joke, but there was truth in it as well. "I've always wanted to help in a bigger way. International law, humanitarian work, foreign journalism, something like that. You and Mom have known that for years."

"It's getting closer to reality now."

"Finally."

"Well, finally for you, but for us, we see our little girl—and we always will. The idea of you in some dangerous war-torn country that probably hates America—that's not very comforting. Your mom wants you to consider other options."

"And what do you think?"

"Maybe I'm blaming your mother for more of this than is fair because, yes, I'd rather see my daughter in a safe career as well. But I also know you have a definite purpose for your life."

"Okay, Dad, we'll talk about it. What about Megan?"

Dad raised his eyebrow, and they both smiled. "If you can get any of Megan's plans out of her, I'll give you a prize. Want some orange juice?"

"After I shower. Be right back," Ellie said and raced upstairs.

The hot water felt good against her skin. Though her run was harder than usual after a week off, the exercise invigorated a renewed strength. She was getting back to her old self. No more thinking that her grandfather might haunt her more in death than in life. That he'd get even for the bracelet, or that he was somehow responsible for her losing it. She didn't believe that, anyway.

She wished life were as easy to clean up as a good scrub in the shower. She believed in finding peace with people, and it nagged at her that Grandfather Edward was gone.

Standing at the cemetery, she had remembered drawing a picture for him when she was seven years old. It showed a little girl with tears dripping to the ground beside a row of flowers. She'd drawn it after Grandfather had yelled at her for something; she couldn't remember what. And across the top she'd written, *Sorry. I love you Grandpa.*

She never gave it to him. She had been too afraid.

Chapter 3

THE OUTSIDER

The Anonymous Blog about Life at West Redding High

Saturday Edition (Why not?)

This blog is getting so many hits that it might indicate that I'm—ugh, no, please, not that—popular. This is "The Outsider," folks, so please read and respond, but don't go around school searching for the writer or looking at him or her (which is me) with some kind of praise and following. And absolutely no voting for me for homecoming queen or king. I'm serious. You will experience pain.

Now back to my thoughts about that, in fact. Homecoming is coming in a few weeks. Someone needs to shine up those tiaras so our homecoming royalty can be sparkly. What is it about homecoming? My intense research, a quick peek on the ever-reliable Wikipedia (that was a joke, folks—do not use Wikipedia for your fact-finding research, though I gotta say that I love it), revealed that homecoming started as a time to welcome back school alumni—the first ones were held at universities in Missouri and Illinois back in the early 1900s. I believe the whole royalty thing was made up by the same kind of people who started beauty pageants. Yes, I find them both disgusting, but is that a surprise? This is "The Outsider"!

And yet, instead of ranting about it, we're going to combat it. We're going to vote for The Outsider Queen and King during homecoming. So start thinking of nominations. The first nomination is for Cappy Bradshaw. Not many at Redding High know him, but he has a photography portfolio that'd blow you away. And since I'm the blogmaster here, I'm giving him 5 votes.

Enjoy your weekend. Don't do anything you wouldn't want told on "The Outsider."

* * *

"You either want to have sex tonight or else you're being cruel to that boyfriend of yours."

Ellie stood before the mirror, putting on eyeliner, as Megan came into the room.

"I like this skirt," Ellie said defensively, turning to the side to see just how short it was. It was short, and she wasn't planning to wear it tonight. She was just trying on different shirts and pants from the clothes she'd grabbed from her occupied room. Now if she changed, Megan would think it was because of her comment.

"Where'd you go last night?" Ellie asked.

"Out." Megan picked up one of Ellie's shirts and gave it a condescending look.

"Do you sneak out often?"

Megan shrugged. "Pretty much."

"How long have you been friends with Will?"

Megan flopped onto her bed and looked at her black fingernail polish. "I don't know. Like our entire lives. Why do you care?"

"I don't care. I just wondered." Ellie looked at her sister through the mirror as she put on mascara. "He said he went to Brazil in fourth grade to live with his grandparents."

"Yeah."

"I had a little crush on him before that." Ellie laughed, thinking of it now. "Then he just disappeared. I thought he didn't like me, 'cause he didn't even say good-bye. Why did he go to Brazil?"

"It's some big long story. Ask him. I don't know why you two can't just talk to each other."

"What do you mean?" Ellie turned around. "He asks things about me?"

"Yeah, sometimes." Megan sounded annoyed. "Why all the Q&A? Are you tired of that boyfriend of yours?"

Ellie turned back to the mirror, taking a Q-tip to wipe away a dot of mascara on her eyelid. "He has a name, you know."

"Does he?"

"He's really nice to you, too, especially since you're mainly rude to him."

"He bores me."

"Who doesn't bore you?"

"Not many people. This conversation is boring me."

Neither of them spoke after that.

Ellie wore her black jeans and a red shirt with loose translucent sleeves that she'd bought at a new shop owned by a local artist/designer. Ellie loved going into Michelle's to wander around and see the latest creations, both clothing and artwork.

A draft at her feet made her decide on boots instead of

open-toed shoes. She grabbed a sweater, thinking it'd be a shame to cover the beautiful sleeves. She took a last look in the mirror. Her dark hair was straightened and shiny and looked fuller than usual. She wiped away a slight smudge of eye shadow. The dark makeup she wore tonight, mainly to cover the circles under her eyes and the fact that she felt fatigued, either looked good or made her look like a hooker— she hoped for the former.

Ryan stopped midstep up the walkway when she opened the door. It wasn't an act, and he tried to hide it. "You look . . . nice," he said in a soft voice.

"Thanks," she said, embarrassed and pleased at the same time. "Where are we going?"

"That's the surprise." Ryan grinned.

"I thought this was a special night, not a surprise night," she said, narrowing her eyes.

"Patience."

"Since I'm such a patient person?" she said with a laugh. Even with her doubt about their future, the way he made her feel lighter and less stressed dispelled her concerns.

They drove north on Interstate 5, then turned off and up a winding road.

"Looks like we're headed toward Shasta Dam," she said. "Are we seeking more structures rising from the lake?"

"Okay, that does it," he said and pulled onto the shoulder. He handed her a black blindfold.

"You're kidding. Where did you get this?"

"I borrowed it from Sam. She made it for the pin-the-tail-on-the-donkey game for her birthday party."

"Nice. I'm sure a six-year-old's blindfold will work great."

"Go ahead." He was serious.

"I'll get carsick if I'm blindfolded."

"We're almost there."

She let him tie it around her head, blocking out the view. She felt a quick peck on the lips. The car moved forward again, and Ellie grabbed the armrest to keep her balance. They went only a few miles and turns before she heard gravel under the tires, and Ryan stopped the car.

"Stay there, but don't take off the blindfold."

He turned off the engine and went outside. She heard the door shut and the trunk open and close, and then her door opened.

"Okay, here we are."

She blinked as he took off her blindfold. Then she saw the pathway of lights.

"What is this?" Small candles glowed from inside two rows of glass containers lined up along the sides of a path.

"Come on." Ryan's expression was sweet and excited. He took her hand, and the touch of his strong fingers woven through hers sent a shiver through her stomach.

"What's that?" she asked, nodding toward the bag on his shoulder.

"Nothing, nothing."

He led her down the short path, tall pines hovering overhead, until they turned a corner. Suddenly the trees opened up, and the trail of candles surrounded a blanket spread out on the ground before a view that stretched out above a huge canyon.

She paused, awestruck. The sun was setting—as if he'd planned even that.

Ryan smiled in satisfaction. "That was the look on your face I was hoping for."

"It's incredible."

"Hurry, let's sit down. We have three minutes before sunset."

"Three minutes? How do you know?"

"Google," he said and motioned for her to sit. The blanket was surprisingly comfortable, and she noticed a pile of rocks off to the side and the crunch of leaves as she sat down. So he'd even provided some cushioning. He'd placed the blanket perfectly with a view of the dam off to the right, the wide Sacramento River streaming far below, and the sun falling fast toward the mountains.

Ryan opened the bag, which turned out to be a sort of picnic basket, and handed her a bottle of San Pellegrino mineral water—her favorite. "Maybe this will cheer up your bad week."

"Bad week?" she said, still in shock over everything he'd done. And for the life of her, she couldn't remember what had been bad. Oh yes, the funeral, and the relatives, and the missing bracelet.

"This is really amazing."

"Don't sound quite so surprised," he said, unzipping another section of the picnic bag. "I have a lot of surprises up my sleeve."

"Well, this was certainly one of them."

"There it goes," Ryan said, watching the sun disappear.

But Ellie was watching Ryan, his strong jaw and perfect lips. This was not a Ryan that most people knew or expected. He was the cool and friendly jock that most everyone loved—

just a good guy who also happened to have a great body and looks, but wasn't especially deep, sensitive, or creative.

"How did you do this?" she asked.

"Well, I had to recruit a little help."

"The guys?" she said in surprise.

"Actually, my mom, Cass, and Sam."

"Really?" Ellie didn't know his mom as well as she should by now. But his little sisters always asked her to come over and play with them when she'd see them at the football games.

I should be totally and completely in love with this guy. And she wanted to be. Perhaps there was some love mechanism broken within her.

They ate crackers with a gourmet spread, olives, sourdough bread, Brie, and slices of Italian salami, Ryan's favorite.

"We've been going out for nearly six months."

Ellie popped an olive into her mouth and nodded.

"What do you think . . . What do you see . . ." He shook his head and laughed. "I'm not saying this very well, am I?"

And Ellie thought, *Please, no, don't ask these things now. Let's enjoy this perfect moment.*

"We have a lot of fun together," Ellie said, and surprised even herself at how lame that sounded. She tried to correct it. "I'm always happy with you."

"Okay," he said, nodding. "So . . ."

"I don't know," Ellie said. "It sort of surprised me when we started going out. We went on the first date after I lost that bet." She smiled. "Then we just kept going out. It still sort of surprises me sometimes."

"Because I wasn't part of your five-year goals." Ryan fiddled with the lid to the olives.

She nodded, laughing. "You might be the most spontaneous thing I've ever done."

"I've thought that was a good thing."

"Me too, actually."

"And I, on the other hand, who usually live on a whim, have been strategic about all of this."

Ellie wondered what that meant. Strategic about getting her, being with her, sleeping with her?

"Why are you with me?" Ryan asked suddenly.

"What does that mean?"

"It's pretty clear."

"I'm with you because . . . because we get along so well, because we have so much fun together." *And*, Ellie thought, *could this be it?* Maybe it should be, if it wasn't going to work anyway. He'd done so much to make tonight special, and now they were so quickly on the brink of ending it.

"I'm ready for more." He stated it clearly, matter-of-factly.

"What more?" *So this is about sex?*

"Everything more. I want to tell you that I love you, and you say the same back. I want to talk about college, maybe try to get into the same one. I want to be with you, get closer, all of it."

And even as Ryan said it, she knew that he knew she wasn't there yet. The nighttime shadows crept around them, and Ellie couldn't distinguish his expression. She shivered, and he noticed.

"No response to that, huh?" He rose quickly and started packing up the bag. "Forget I said it, then."

Ellie stood and picked up their drinks. She needed to say something. But what could she say that wouldn't hurt him?

He'd seemed happy in their relationship. Why change it, when changing it only seemed to point one way?

They carried the bag and blanket back to the car; then Ryan turned and marched back down the trail. All she could see was the trail of candles disappearing one at a time, and something about it transfixed her until he returned.

"You know how easily I could get someone else?" he said.

"Oh, that's nice. Classic Ryan."

"And what does that mean?"

She shook her head and got into the car. "Why don't you just fit right into the jock stereotype?"

He closed the trunk and got into the driver's seat, turning on the engine. "I've already lived the stereotype."

"Well, maybe I don't want to be another of your 'been there, done that' girls."

"Is that what you think?"

"I don't know what I think."

Neither spoke as the car idled softly. An old love song played, something from Aerosmith.

"I shouldn't have said that." Ryan rested his elbows on the steering wheel.

She loved his arms, the perfect contour of muscle and the smoothness of his skin.

"It's just not easy having a girlfriend who isn't really into me."

Ellie felt a sting of guilt. How could she explain it to him?

"Ryan, there are so many places I want to see and so much work I want to do. This place pulls you in and keeps people. My dad had all these dreams once, and look at him."

"What's wrong with your dad? He teaches kids, probably makes a huge impact in their lives."

"He didn't do anything that he wanted."

"Is he unhappy?"

Ellie paused then. "I don't know. I don't think so, but—"

"I know a lot of people who do go after what they want, and they aren't happy."

"A lot of people? Like who?"

"My mom, her sister, my dad. And others. You want me to name them all? They're all successful."

"And they regret it?"

"No, probably not, I'm sure not. But they aren't happy either. Success isn't the gauge of happiness."

"I know that," she said, suddenly aggravated. She was the one who talked about the dangers of success, that success was in giving and living a life of meaning. She organized the fund-raisers. She'd gone to Mexico over the summer and helped build a mission. Ryan followed her around at times and volunteered, but that was because he wanted to be with her, not to do the work. And now he was defending what he knew nothing about.

She wanted to tell him. But the words were too heavy, and none of it really mattered. They were coming to the end. There'd be awkwardness for a while. He was her first real boyfriend, after all. And he claimed he'd never told anyone else "I love you."

She'd miss him, too, miss so many things about him. His strength, and the way she could sit beside him in his Mustang with the music on and feel completely safe and protected from the world outside. She'd miss their easy laughter and the stories he told. She'd miss when he got serious, which was rare, and the way he would talk about things she didn't think he told anyone else. His hand on her chin. His way of taking away her intensity . . .

But she wouldn't have to battle his desire for her. And though her body reacted and at times longed greatly for more of his hands and more of his lips, she didn't want him to be her first. Ellie had made commitments to herself, and she wasn't going to break them in a weak moment.

He leaned his head on the steering wheel. "Do you still want to go to the party?"

"I never did want to go."

"Then what do you want to do?"

She shrugged her shoulders. "Let's just go to the party."

"Fine."

* * *

Megan glanced at James onstage as he moved his fingers over the strings of the guitar. Musicians. Why was she heading down this road again? Her six tumultuous months with Kyle the Drummer ended with the inevitable cheating. He'd said sleeping with groupies shouldn't count since they didn't mean anything to him. Then his bandmate tried to "comfort" her, which started an all-band fight. Megan and Kyle weren't the only thing that broke up that night.

"So what do you think?" Naomi asked over the noise of the band.

Megan leaned in to get a closer view of Naomi's newest lip piercing. It was red around the edges. She nodded approval.

"This one didn't hurt at all. When's your turn?"

"One month," Megan said, then glanced again at James as if she barely noticed him.

Their eyes connected, and he gave a slight nod and smile. This wasn't going to turn out good, but Megan suddenly didn't care. Not all musicians were made alike, right?

"I thought you swore off men." Naomi took a drink of her rum and Coke.

"Not men per se."

"Just men with drumsticks or microphones or—what's that in his hand?—guitars."

The waitress came by and asked if anyone wanted anything, but Megan shook her head.

When the band took a break, Megan watched James from the corner of her eye as he approached the bar. A few minutes later, he set two beers on the table, then turned the chair around and sat down. "Wanna get out of here later?" he asked.

Megan shrugged. "Yeah, why not?"

* * *

Ellie paused at the door. She glanced at Ryan and nearly apologized and asked to go somewhere to talk. But then she touched the doorbell and someone yelled from inside, "It's about time!"

The door flew open, and Ryan was quickly pulled into the kitchen, where a gang of guys cheered his arrival. Ellie looked toward the living room, where some girls from school were sitting and motioning her over.

"This is a segregated party—boys in the kitchen," Stasia said with a smile.

"It looks that way."

"We were about to bet on whether you were coming or not," Heather said. "Mitch was sure you guys were coming by."

"Yeah, I'm usually too much of a Goody Two-shoes," Ellie said, getting a laugh from Stasia and another girl, Nikki, who sat on the couch.

Heather sat on the edge of the coffee table and barely smiled. She was Tara's sidekick and had taken on an air of snobbery toward everyone else, which was somewhat humorous since they'd known her since kindergarten. There was no impressing people who once pushed you on a swing or shared a mat with you at naptime.

Ellie noticed an older guy out on the patio, watching her through the window.

"That's Mitch's father," Nikki said. "Yuck."

Ellie agreed; it creeped her out the way he was watching them. She sat in a chair out of his view. The party seemed mellow and relaxed, probably because a number of people were stoned. They came in from around the pool with the scent of pot surrounding them like the rings of Saturn. Ellie tried to act natural, but this was only her second party in her entire high school experience. The first had been a wild kegger some guy from student council had taken her to, and she'd asked to leave a few minutes into it.

"Whoa, cool, it's Ellie," said one of the guys.

Nikki took a drink from a plastic cup. "Want something?"

Through the arched opening to the kitchen, Ellie could see that Ryan was involved in some kind of beer-drinking game. "No, I think I'll be driving tonight," she said.

"Looks like it," Heather said.

Ellie didn't want to be here. She wanted to go home and figure out what had happened with Ryan tonight.

But Stasia was talking to her, asking, "Where are you going next year, Ellie? Do you know?"

"I'm not sure yet," Ellie said, and that wasn't fully a lie. She had to get accepted to Stanford to go there.

Stasia was planning to start at Shasta College so she could continue working at her dad's accounting firm and save money. Nikki wanted to be a dental hygienist. Heather didn't tell her plans, and Ellie wondered if she should ask where her BFF Tara was going and if Heather was following. For a while they talked about snowboarding and the best places to go if Mount Shasta didn't open until late again.

Ellie did her best to participate in the conversation.

"He won't wait forever, you know," Heather said when she noticed Ellie watching Ryan in the kitchen. He kept looking out the doorway to where she sat, though they pretended not to notice each other.

"What do you mean?"

"Your boyfriend. He's Ryan, probably the most popular guy at school. He has girls waiting and willing to take him off your hands, since you don't seem to want him that badly. They'd be willing and waiting regardless—some girls are just that way." Heather smirked.

"Girls like Tara?" Ellie asked.

Heather laughed slightly. "Tara could have him if she wanted him."

"Oh, she could?" Stasia said, crossing her arms and leaning forward.

Ellie had always liked Stasia, even if they weren't usually in the same circles.

"No offense, Ellie," Heather said.

"Why do you hang out with her?" Nikki said. "She walks around with this attitude like *I'm a porn star beneath my Gucci clothes.*"

Heather laughed. "Like I said, she could have Ryan if she wanted him."

"Don't listen to her," Stasia said. "Seriously. Why don't you shut up, Heather?"

But the seed was there, the doubt, the wonder. Ryan was looking at her again, and this time their eyes caught and held for a moment before his friends called his name and he turned away.

It was over. Ellie knew it, and surely he did too. And yet anger coursed through her at Heather's words. Ryan loved her. Not even a porn star in Gucci could take that away, right?

Heather knew she'd rattled Ellie; it was written in her smug expression.

"Hey, let's get a drink," Stasia said, taking Ellie's hand. Ellie followed her to the kitchen, where the guys cheered loudly in front of a beer bong. Bly—the usual victim—was sitting passed out in a chair with a top hat on his head and a mustache drawn above his lip.

"When are you leaving?" Ellie asked.

Stasia smiled with understanding. "I could go now."

"But have you been drinking?"

"Water," she said with a smile. "I have diabetes, so alcohol is out."

Ryan came up to Ellie and put his arm around her shoulders. "Are you okay?" he asked.

"I'm catching a ride with Stasia."

"Why?" He held a half-empty beer bottle in his hand.

Since they started dating, Ryan had pretty much stopped drinking with his friends. Ellie hadn't asked him to, but he said that being with her made him want a better life. She thought of how happy he'd been with his sunset picnic just hours earlier, and her heart ached for him. She'd hurt him. But she didn't know how to make it better right now.

"I'm really tired, Ryan. Why don't I have Stasia take us both home?"

"I don't need a ride. I'll be fine."

He was drunk, or close to it. Ellie told Stasia to wait a minute so she could find someone to either help Ryan go with her or assure her that they'd take care of him. She walked past a couple making out in a chair and finally spotted Tank outside with Mitch's creepy dad. Tank was smoking a giant cigar, and Mitch's dad rose from his chair when he saw Ellie.

"I'm taking you home." Ryan was behind her.

"No, you aren't."

"I'm fine. And I want to take you. This was our date. So let me drive you home. I just want to ask you something."

Ellie poked her head out the door and called, "Tank, would you help, please?"

"Els." Ryan pulled at her arm, drawing her back inside.

Tank quickly took in the situation. He came over and put his arm around Ryan. "What's going on, man?"

"I need to take Els home."

"Listen, man, you aren't going. Get over it. We won't let you drive like this."

"Do you need a ride home?" Mitch's dad asked, his eyes glancing over Ellie.

"I have a ride, thanks," she said, looking around for Stasia.

"Els!" Ryan called.

"Man, let's get you to a chair," Tank said, leading Ryan toward the living room.

"Els, why don't you love me?"

The room's volume dropped dramatically low. Everyone looked at her, and then Ryan was there, taking her hands.

Ellie looked into his eyes and said softly, "Let's talk about this tomorrow, Ryan, okay?"

"But I want to know now."

His friends surrounded them. "We can get him."

"I've got to get Els home," he said as they pulled him toward the backyard door. "You know, Els, you don't open up. You're closed off—people don't know that. You're so nice and understanding. But who do you let understand you?"

Ellie stood there, unable to move. Her face turned hot with embarrassment, even as she wondered if maybe he was right. Who did she confide in?

"I'll take you home," Mitch's dad said, trying to lead her toward the front door.

"Ready?" Stasia stood in the doorway, hands on her hips. She gave Mitch's dad a death stare.

"Yes," Ellie said.

They walked out of the house and down the walkway. They heard a noise behind them and turned to see Ryan stumble and fall over a hedge and into a flower bed. Tank jumped in to pull him back out, and Kevin hurried over to help. They carried Ryan into the house.

Kevin called, "He'll be okay. Just get out of here."

"Sure?" Ellie asked. She didn't know if she should stay, but she really wanted to go, and quickly.

"Yeah, we'll keep him here."

"Thanks."

Stasia and Ellie turned from the house and started down the driveway.

"Maybe I should take his car." That would ensure that Ryan wouldn't escape and drive off, though that was more of a boyfriend/girlfriend thing to do. Tonight had probably ended that status.

"They'll take care of him," Stasia reassured her. "You okay?"

"Yeah. Thanks for this."

"No problem. Why I came to this thing in the first place, I have no idea."

"It was boring anyway," Ellie said.

"Yeah, 'cause you don't drink. And I can't drink. Or at least, I can't drink enough to enjoy the party, only enough to make me tired."

"I didn't know you had diabetes."

"Since I was twelve."

Ellie followed Stasia down the driveway, wishing she had Ryan's jacket.

"I had to park sort of far," Stasia said as she typed into her cell phone.

The heels of Ellie's shoes clomped along the driveway. Stasia had come to the party dressed in jeans and a sweatshirt and running shoes. Her hair was in a ponytail, which only served to make her round face appear rounder.

Stasia was one of those pretty girls the guys wouldn't notice until they were older, Ellie thought. Or like in a teen movie when the girl who was always the "friend" suddenly had a makeover or came home from college, and all the guys went crazy. That could be Stasia. Ellie remembered going to one of her birthday parties when they were little. Stasia had been into horses back then. Ellie wondered if she still was.

Stasia pointed ahead. "Look. The neighbors are going to love that." There was a beer can tower at the entrance to Mitch's driveway. "Wow, I can't believe the cops haven't come."

Stasia's car was a four-door Honda, red with silver rims.

"Cute car," Ellie said.

"It's not as cute as yours."

Ellie laughed. Her green Karmann Ghia was an adorable wreck. "It's broken down half the time. There's something to be said for a car that's less than twenty years old. But I had to have it."

"You know, Ellie, Ryan will call you tomorrow."

Ellie shrugged, glancing behind them and pulling her sweater closer around her chest. "I think it might be over anyway."

"Seriously? Why?"

"I don't know. We see everything so differently. In the beginning maybe I was flattered that he liked me."

"Why would *you* be flattered?"

Ellie laughed. "'Cause I don't have a ton of guys knocking at my door."

"Don't give me that. Now, I don't have *any* guys knocking at my door. The guys see me as their sporty little sister."

She clicked the key fob to unlock the doors, and they hopped into the car. The leather seats were cold.

The heater blew cold air, and Ellie felt the chill down to her bones. Ryan hadn't come after her, and of course, in his state of being, he shouldn't. Still, she felt a longing to see him rush toward her—the Ryan she knew so well, not the drunk one—and wrap his arms around her, tell her it was going to be okay. Instead, she'd left him. Left him when he needed her most.

Stasia adjusted the heater vent, looked at Ellie, and asked, "You okay?"

"Yeah."

"He'll be fine. He'll be embarrassed, but fine. It will be better."

Ellie nodded, but she didn't believe it. These were supposedly the best years of life—or so her Uncle Henry always said with a wistful look in his eyes. *Enjoy these times, Elspeth. They're the best. Simply the best.*

Stasia turned on the radio—it was playing country music. "Why are you ending it with Ryan?"

"I'm not. Or maybe I am." Ellie didn't want to talk about it. Ryan would say that was because she didn't like to open up. "You know," she said, changing the subject, "we should hang out more."

Stasia smiled as she drove down the road. "We should. High school is so crazy. I don't really do much with any of my friends anymore. Life's short, so we should enjoy it."

"Exactly."

The heater warmed slowly from the first blasts of cold. Ellie would take a hot bath when she got home; maybe she'd even light candles. The aunts were leaving in the morning. Her well-organized life could get fully back on schedule. In a few months she'd start applying to colleges. In a year she'd be settled nicely into university life and pursuing the studies she anxiously waited for: political science, international studies . . . Maybe she'd go abroad her second or third year, at least for a semester—France or Japan or Italy.

"I didn't hear what you wanted to major in," Ellie said.

"I don't know. I like little kids, so I think about teaching. My mom wants me to follow in my dad's footsteps and become a CPA—I am good with numbers. But I doubt I'll know for a while. You didn't fool me in there. I bet you already have your future pretty well planned."

Ellie smiled. "Not exactly. I'd like to eventually be the head of a humanitarian organization or something in international law to stop war crimes." Ellie didn't usually tell people the extent of her plans, but Stasia seemed like someone who could hear it without thinking she was aspiring too high. "Maybe even run for office, though Ryan says I'm too nice for politics."

Ellie typed Vanessa a text:

I think Ryan and I just broke up. Sorry, I know you
wanted the homecoming thing.

"We could use a few nice people in politics. Where are you going next year?" Stasia asked.

"Stanford, I think. I hope. Depends on a lot of things

though." Her voice drifted off as they saw flashing red lights ahead.

"Looks like an accident," Stasia said.

An ambulance was parked to the side, and three highway patrol cars were at different angles off the road, with lights on, one flashing. A spotlight shone on the back end of a truck that was down the embankment and at the river's edge. An EMT was in the back of the truck, while several police officers leaned in through the side windows.

"Can you see anything?" Stasia asked, craning her neck as they drove by.

Ellie strained to see what was happening. "Not much. One paramedic is looking in through the back window. I can't see anyone though."

"Scary," Stasia said. "Hope it isn't anyone from the party."

Ellie glanced over at her and then back toward the truck. She pictured it being Ryan down there, which of course was impossible. "I don't recognize the truck."

They continued forward, and the lights of the accident disappeared behind them. Ellie was glad that neither of them had taken a drink. Sobriety checks were common in Redding on the weekends now. Stasia was telling about an accident her brother had been in the year before as a song by Foreigner came on. "Waiting for a Girl Like You"—it was one of Ryan's favorites, and he'd sing it out loud when they drove.

A text beeped on her phone.

Vanessa: No way! Why? What happened?

The road grew dark again as they went through a long

stretch of country with few cars. Stasia reached for the stereo. "I'm not an Elvis fan."

"Watch out!" Ellie yelled as a deer ran across the road. The
deer paused in the stream of the headlights. Stasia cranked
the wheel and hit the brakes. The car turned sharp, too
sharp, and Stasia tried to turn it back. Ellie put her hands on
the dashboard and caught a look of shock on Stasia's face.

Then the world was whirling around. The sound of metal
crunching and someone screaming. They were turning over
and over. Ellie felt like an outside observer, yet something in
her head said this was her, this was really happening.

Then just as suddenly, it was silent, but not really silent.
Eerie quiet surrounded them. The heater was still running,
but the engine wasn't. Ellie didn't know if they were upside
down or what. Stasia's car was upended, scattering everything. Chapstick, money, receipts, a stuffed animal of some
kind. She couldn't find her purse or her cell phone.

"Stasia?" she called in a little voice, maybe no voice at all.
"Stasia!"

There was no answer, but Ellie heard a vehicle pulling up.
Her cell phone rang, Ryan's ringtone, but the song came from
outside the car.

Light beamed through the back window, and she heard
voices outside. Someone was calling 911.

Ellie couldn't get her arm to move. It was stuck, and
something felt wrong. She couldn't move, and there was pain
from somewhere echoing through her like the long call of a
train's whistle in the deep of night.

Soon people were yelling outside the car. But it was like
she and Stasia were inside a shell, stuck inside with the others

outside. And Stasia wouldn't answer. Ellie couldn't see her either.

"Help!" Ellie cried, and then she caught the scent of smoke. Why wasn't Stasia answering? Why wasn't she calling back? Ellie's right hand crept along her stomach, following the seat belt till she reached the buckle. Pushing with all her strength, she released it with a click. Ellie fell forward, which meant the car had come to rest facing downward. Maybe it was stuck on something or going off an incline.

Then Ellie saw Stasia. Something was wrong with her. She wasn't conscious, and there was blood trailing down her face.

The scent of smoke grew stronger, clogging her lungs, making her cough. Ellie thought how strange and unexpected it was to die right in the middle of life like this, yet it wasn't nearly as scary and terrible as everyone would think.

And just as instantly, she thought how this couldn't be real. She'd been living her life and going along, and now it was over?

People were shouting right outside the window. She reached for them and realized the glass was gone.

"It's going to be okay," someone shouted to her, taking her hand, while another person was yelling frantically.

"It's two girls! One's awake. We gotta get the fire out. Does anyone have a crowbar?"

"Throw dirt on the fire!"

Ellie started coughing, and she fought to free her body.

"We've got to get them out! They won't make it. We gotta get them out now!"

Chapter 4

THE OUTSIDER
The Anonymous Blog about Life at West Redding High
October 19

Comments:

Does anyone know what happened? Someone told me that two girls from Redding High were in an accident and one of them is dead.

I heard it was two girls from Riverside not Redding.

Where's the Outsider?

It was Stasia and Ellie. But I think they're both okay.

No, I heard it was Ellie and Ryan.

It was Stasia by herself.

Ellie got a ride home from Stasia, someone said.

Heather's dad works for the fire department. He said it was two girls, but he didn't tell Heather who. One girl is dead and another in critical condition. But it was a red Honda. That's Stasia's car.

* * *

The call was from Dad. Megan said hello just as she thought it strange that he'd call so late, especially when he believed she was staying the night at Lu's. Dad couldn't know she was at James's apartment that he shared with three other guys. Naomi and the drummer were off in a room, and she and James would already be "checking out his old album collection" in his room except that James and Will had started talking about Bob Dylan.

"Meg, your sister was in a car accident."

Oh, brother was her first thought. Then Megan tried to think what kind of car Ellie could be driving. Wasn't her car broken down again? The sister who had to have a clunker old Karmann Ghia because it looked fun. That car was something *she* would like, not Ellie. Ellie belonged in a four-door, safety-tested Volvo or an ecofriendly Smart car.

"Meg? Are you there? Stay calm, okay?" Dad's voice again.

She almost laughed at how funny he sounded. She tried to focus, but it wasn't easy to think. Her mind moved in slow motion.

"Can you meet us at the hospital?"

That brought the concern and clarity. "Why? Have you talked to her? What happened?"

"Megan, it's bad. It's very bad."

She couldn't move then.

James leaned over. "What is it? What's wrong?"

Will was sitting on a couch across from her. The coffee table was covered with empty beer bottles, a bong, and a bag of weed. "I had a text earlier that someone was in an accident."

"Ellie," Megan said, trying to know that this was really happening.

"I'll drive you," Will said.

They met her parents hurrying out of the emergency room.

"They're taking her to Davis," Dad said. "To the burn center."

"The burn center?" Megan asked, but her voice was drowned by the sound of a helicopter taking off. "Is that her?"

Dad could only nod. Mom looked like she should sit or be admitted herself.

"What happened?"

"We don't know. She was riding home with Stasia Fuller."

"What? Where was Ryan?"

Will stepped up then. "How bad is it, Mr. Summerfield?"

The look on her father's face sobered Megan up.

"Stasia died in the crash." Dad shook his head and started to cry.

Megan had never seen Dad cry, not ever.

"And they don't know if Ellie's going to make it."

Chapter 5

THE OUTSIDER

The Anonymous Blog about Life at West Redding High

October 20

Comments:

The newspaper said they were investigating what happened. They'd been at a party, so it doesn't take a genius.

They weren't drinking. People from the party even said so.

They saw Stasia with a drink. But not Ellie.

Why was Ellie riding with Stasia then?

* * *

"We didn't break up."

Megan looked toward the waiting room and saw Ryan emerge from inside. He turned toward her in the hall, then walked the opposite way, but not before she saw the look on his face. She nearly called to him, but he was already near the end of the corridor.

Vanessa poked her head out of the waiting room, calling, "Ryan, I'm sorry." Then she saw Megan.

No, don't come talk to me.

Vanessa approached her.

That a group of Ellie's friends had driven down to sit in

the waiting room in Davis was beyond annoying. They only added to the agony of this entire ordeal as they sat around chatting about random things, texting on their phones, crying as they talked about her sister. She wanted them all to leave. Megan understood why Ryan was there. And maybe Vanessa. But there were, like, ten other people, a few teachers, the principal, and two pastors from their church. The waiting room was smaller than her bedroom.

"Should I have told him?" Vanessa asked, pulling her hair into a ponytail and wrapping a band around it.

"You're asking me if, while in the hospital waiting room, you should have told Ryan that his girlfriend had broken up with him before she was in a serious car crash that may cost her life and that he blames himself for?" *Are you really that blonde?*

"All I said was sorry about them breaking up. I was trying to make him feel better. He wanted to see the text."

Megan shook her head. This was not a conversation she cared about right now. "Did she say that she actually broke up with him?"

"You read it."

> I think Ryan and I just broke up. Sorry, I know you wanted the homecoming thing.

Seeing what were perhaps her sister's last words printed out on Vanessa's ridiculously bright pink phone sent a sharp jab of pain through Megan. And what last words were they? Ellie was worried that Vanessa would be mad at her. She was saying sorry over stupid homecoming.

"Listen, I don't care about this. But for the record, she didn't say they broke up. The words *I think* are sort of the clue there. So leave me alone. I just care if Ellie lives through the night." Megan unleashed a few profanities under her breath.

That got rid of Vanessa, though Megan felt a strange compulsion to hold on to the cell phone, to hold on to something of her sister. Vanessa's heels clicked down the hall. Seriously, who wore heels to the hospital when her best friend might die?

That Vanessa was Ellie's "best friend" had been just another irrational thing in Ellie's life that no one else seemed to recognize. While everyone thought Ellie was always reaching beyond and above, Megan felt she reached the wrong way. It was hard to admit, but her sister could have been even more.

The hospital sounds returned as Vanessa disappeared— someone moaned in a room, machines beeped, an announcement came over the intercom. Megan stood alone in the hall. Her parents were filling out paperwork. The cold and sterility surrounded her; fluorescent lights hurt her eyes. Ellie was in surgery in some room beyond the double doors. While Megan was smoking and drinking, Ellie had ridden home with a sober driver. Yet Ellie was the one severely burned with her life in jeopardy.

* * *

Megan woke from a dream where she and Ellie were talking.

"*We're just different. That's why we hate each other.*"

"*But I don't hate you,*" Ellie said.

Megan was trying to explain that they did in fact hate

each other on the surface, but underneath they knew they'd always be there for one another. They'd formed a bond as little girls that wouldn't be broken by parental stupidity, a grandfather's favoritism and cruelty, school popularity and shunnings, or anything else.

She awoke in the middle of this dissertation with her neck aching. Several others slept around the waiting room. One girl was texting on her iPhone. Megan headed to the bathroom and then to the cafeteria.

"Here." She set a Styrofoam cup of coffee and a large number of cream and sugar packets on the table in front of Ryan, who sat alone at a table in the corner.

"Thanks," he said, rubbing bloodshot eyes.

She took a red stirry-thingie from the front pocket of her purse and set it down by the cup.

"When do they expect some news?" he asked, and Megan realized it had been only four hours since she'd seen him leave the waiting room. It felt like days.

"The surgeon will be out in about an hour, the nurse said."

Ryan looked at the wall clock and nodded. He sipped his coffee without adding anything, staring at the table. "I was about to go to the chapel."

Megan wondered if that was an invitation or a good-bye.

He hesitated. "Wanna come?"

She shrugged her shoulders. "It's better than the waiting room."

The chapel was just a small, empty room with a row of benches, a carpeted platform, and a wooden altar. On one side was a table with red candles. Only one was lit. Megan had expected something more chapelesque, like stained glass and an ornate altar.

Ryan walked to the table and lit a candle. She saw him close his eyes a moment. His dark brown hair was sticking up, and his T-shirt was wrinkled, jeans baggy. Even if he was a jock, Megan had to admit he was handsome. He was also broken. He found a place on a bench close to the front and seemed to forget that she was there.

Megan didn't know where to sit. By him, behind, or should she just go?

"You can sit here if you want," he said, glancing back at her.

She slid into the bench beside him. "If you want to be alone, just tell me."

He shook his head and ran his hands through his hair. "No, it's okay."

They sat in silence. Ryan leaned forward with his forehead resting on the back of the bench in front of them. Megan felt the quiet settle around them like a peace interrupting the noise. It carefully pushed out the distractions of Vanessa and friends in the waiting room, the distress in her mother's face—though she continued to act hospitable to everyone, as if they'd come to a party at her house—and the family members who kept calling Megan's phone for updates, as if all of this were easier on her than on Mom or Dad.

"I wonder if God gets sick of people only talking to Him when they're desperate," Ryan said, leaning back beside her. His eyes were on the empty wall above the carpeted altar area.

Megan didn't really want to think about God. She sometimes went to church if Mom begged long enough. There had been God discussions at parties. She'd thought about becoming a Buddhist for a while, but that was more to upset the family than to actually seek enlightenment. Long ago, she had loved Jesus. But that love seemed far, far away now. "If I were God, I would. But maybe not, since He's, you know, God and all."

"I thought you didn't believe in God."

Megan glanced around nervously. "You shouldn't say that while we're in a chapel."

He glanced at her with an eyebrow raised.

"I'm not really an atheist. I told Ellie that so she'd stop inviting me to youth group. She was driving me crazy."

Ryan smiled then. "She always invited me too. I only went sometimes, to see her." His smile faded. "We got in a fight before the party."

Megan shrugged. "People get in fights."

"We didn't break up. Vanessa got a text from Els saying we might have broken up or something like that. So she tells that to everyone."

Megan closed her eyes. The pain radiated from Ryan. He really did love her sister. As in, really *loved*. Megan had always thought of him as another dumb athlete, and maybe he was that, though he was surprising her a lot in just the short time she'd been talking to him.

"If she doesn't make it through this . . ."

Megan wanted to say, "She will." But the truth was, Megan didn't know that. The realization hit like a slap to her face.

"If I had driven her home . . . I should have taken her

home . . . or we never should have gone to Mitch's." Ryan shook his head and spoke quietly, not with self-pity but with such a burden of guilt.

Megan could think of nothing to say that could make it better. So she closed her eyes again. And before long, she was asking God for help whether it annoyed Him or not. They needed it. For Ellie, for Stasia's family, and for each of them as well.

Chapter 6

THE OUTSIDER
The Anonymous Blog about Life at West Redding High
November 1

Comments:

What's happening on "The Outsider"?

Can anyone find out more about Ellie? I heard she was burned in the fire. It's been a week. Who went to Stasia's memorial?

I nominate Erica Howe for Outsider Homecoming Queen. She's a pianist at the senior center.

You can't nominate yourself, Erica.

I went to Stasia's memorial. It was really sad.

Where's the Outsider?

I don't know, but on Redding Higher blog they have a bunch more info.

* * *

The beep sounded again. Annoying, rhythmic, constant. Like Chinese water torture. A clock made a *tick, tick* sound. Voices came through the fog like poison darts hitting her unsuspectedly, bringing a dull pain that grew so sharp and heavy she wanted to scream.

"She's awake. I think she's awake."

"No, she's not awake."

Then a familiar woman's voice was whispering, but was nearly hysterical. Was it Mom?

"Her eyes are moving. Ellie, can you hear me? Does that mean she's dreaming? Dreaming must be good. It means her brain . . . is okay."

"Jane, she's going to be okay. All of her will be."

The conversation might have been entertaining, except that each word spoken by whoever was in the room was too loud, too painful against her body that felt ripped into a million tiny shreds. She couldn't get to them either, to hear who they were talking about, to tell them to be quiet, someone was trying to sleep here.

Go away, Ellie tried to say.

"She *is* awake!" someone said, and there was movement and rustling that echoed away like a slow falling down into darkness.

* ✳ *

Time had passed. Ellie could sense this as she tried to open eyes that were weighted down with something. But where was she? What were the sounds she heard but couldn't see?

Ellie and her sister were playing in a blue plastic swimming pool. Ellie liked to lie flat on her back under the water and open her eyes. She could see the trees and sky through the shimmering water. Then her sister brought the hose, and water gushed from the end, erupting her sight into a whirling scene. And again, she was being sucked from that light toward darkness.

PAIN . . .

PAIN.

PAIN!

It screamed in her ears, a white-hot light in her eyes. Her brain was on fire. She was on fire. The world was on fire. *God, help me . . .*

It woke her again like a raging bull with its horns on fire.

Pain.

Fiery hot, searing, screaming, mind expanding and contracting. Everything in her was on fire. A car was burning, and there were people around her now, doctors and nurses with masks over their faces and their eyes staring at something below her, and then also above her. And they wouldn't put her out. She tried to scream and flail around, but they held her there, pouring liquid fire, cutting with molten tools, searing off her body.

"We have to do this, Ellie," someone said.

The pain was eternal. The lake of fire for all eternity. All her praying, her life for God, and she'd gone wrong. It was all wrong. She was in hell, and people just watched her. She was in hell for believing the wrong God or for being a failure or for something she'd done wrong.

Jesus, Jesus, where are You? God, somebody, anybody, help me. Make them stop!

"Mom!" she cried, and Mom was there with a mask over her face, and she was crying too.

"Sweetie, you'll be okay. They're going to make you better."

"Don't let them hurt me anymore."

The cycle continued. When she was not in the depths of darkness, pain filled her being. It woke her and coursed through her like acid in her veins.

There was something going on outside. Pain was there, eating at her, ripping away her body. Ellie could feel every bit of it, and yet, strangely, she was somewhat safe deep down in this place she'd found. She'd been in an accident. She was in a hospital; she'd figured that out from the brief passing times of consciousness that brought her voices and blurred images.

Sometimes in her head Ellie thought of funny things to say to people. Finally she had the chance to think them up in advance. People would laugh, she knew. But then later, she couldn't remember them, or the memories, or anything much at all.

Then Ryan was there, and Ellie realized he'd been there before. Mostly it had been her parents and nurses and doctors. But right now, she was sure of it, Ryan was there with her. She could hear his voice.

There was no hand-holding, touching her chin, or leaning her head on his shoulder. Ellie could only open her right eye for some reason, and that took such effort.

A chair was pulled up by her bedside. But a screen divided them. He was shimmery behind plastic, like she was once again looking at the world from beneath the water. She put her hand to the plastic, and Ryan appeared anxious and happy but worried suddenly.

She tried to tell him something. He came closer, pressing up against the plastic until it distorted his face.

"Remember . . ." Ellie said.

"What?" he asked with a look of panic.

She formed the words in her head, seeing the letters of each as though she were typing a text message. With the greatest effort, she said the words again. "Re-mem-ber. No or-gan mu-sic."

She thought he might laugh, which she wanted before falling back to sleep. The darkness was pulling her back down like a feather falling gently to earth. But there was no laughing. He was crying. He was sobbing with his hand over his mouth and his head on the edge of the bed. If only she could lift her hand and set it on his head, tell him she was kidding, that she was fine.

Why didn't he laugh? she wondered halfway down inside the deep place. And it struck her like a wicked blow that sent her toppling end over end. She was worse off than she knew.

He didn't laugh because it wasn't a joke.

Chapter 7

egan tied the mask that covered her mouth, completing her surgical outfit before the nurse motioned her toward the door. She paused a moment, then forced her feet to move forward.

For the past two weeks she'd avoided this moment. When her turn to go into Ellie's room had come, she'd let Ryan go instead, even if only family was supposed to be allowed. They'd said he was her brother. She wanted to see her sister, and she didn't want to see her.

Mom always came out crying. She'd been given little white pills to get her through the days. Dad hugged Megan constantly now, and it was driving her crazy.

She was sick of this place with all the hushed discussion, hugging, tears, and sterile, harshly lit halls and waiting rooms. She was sick of hospital food. She'd gotten so sick of the disgusted looks of passersby when she had sneaked out to smoke that she'd tossed her cigarettes into the trash. Now her hands felt shaky, and she realized that she really had become hooked on the stupid "cancer sticks"—as Grandfather had called them as he lit one for her.

She stood at the door. The room was cold and nearly empty of furnishings. There were machines, wires and tubes, a pumping noise and beeping sounds. Everything was focused on the body on the bed draped with a plastic cover. The body that wasn't moving, only lying there like something from a sci-fi movie. The body that was her sister.

Megan took careful steps forward, as if she might wake Ellie, or as if she were approaching a corpse.

Ellie wasn't conscious, whether from the pain medication or the accident, Megan didn't know. She hadn't been fully conscious since the accident.

And then Megan saw Ellie's face, but it couldn't be Ellie—it looked nothing like her. Her hand went to her already covered mouth. She'd come to talk to her sister and to tell her that everything was okay and that she'd soon be back to her old self again.

But Megan couldn't say anything. She stared, with her hand near her masked mouth. This couldn't be her sister. They'd made a mistake. Her face was swollen, and one side was covered in thick gel. That side was the worst, with blisters and cuts and fierce wounds so disgusting Megan thought she might vomit. But the other side, though swollen, could be recognized as Ellie when she really looked. And the hair was the right color.

There was a lone chair by the bed. She forced her feet to it, one step after another. Sitting down, Megan decided to look at her sister's right arm and hand that had only a few scrapes and Ellie's perfect skin. She breathed deeply to calm herself, but the smell in the room made her ill. It was medicinal and smelled of burnt flesh.

"Hey, Ellie," she whispered. "It's Megan. Bet you didn't expect me. It's true; they called in the big sister."

Tears were falling from her eyes as she carefully reached for her sister's hand. She remembered how, as a little girl, Ellie always wanted to hold her hand, but Megan didn't like it. Ellie liked to watch TV with her head on Megan's shoulder, and she'd sneak into bed with Megan, too, which was something Megan did like because she was a little afraid of the dark. Mom had pictures of them as two little girls curled together asleep.

"You're going to be okay. Before you know it, you'll be back to school with your schedule all organized, planning some fund-raiser. So keep fighting, okay? I'll come back soon."

And she hurried out.

Megan couldn't breathe, but pushed her feet to move past Dad, who called after her, and all the way to the first exit she could find.

She closed her eyes, bent down as she gasped for the fresh air to fill her lungs.

Someone once said that Megan was more of an exotic beauty, while Ellie was fresh faced and natural, whatever that meant. Guys often found Megan attractive and her sarcastic demeanor intimidating or intriguing. Usually guys who expected things went after her.

But what would it be like to really be naturally beautiful? To go running or wake in the morning and still look pretty? Megan wouldn't know, but Ellie lived that every day. Or had. What would it be like to have your beauty taken away?

* * *

"We thought we lost you," Ellie heard her dad say.

The sound of someone crying came from farther off.

"Mom, you can't keep crying when you come in here. It's not good for her."

Megan's voice. So that would be her mother crying.

The more she woke, the more pain pulsated through her. Ellie wanted to go back to the safety of sleep or unconsciousness—it didn't matter what it was, just anything away from the pain.

"Let her rest," Mom said between sobs.

"The doctor said to start waking her up. Talking to her."

Megan again, scolding Mom with her tone.

The room came into focus. White everything, then shapes, then faces. The people wore medical gowns and hats. The people were her family. Her mother was sobbing from the corner. Her sister stood near the door, biting her nails and staring at her.

Don't bite your nails, Megan, she wanted to say.

"Do you know what happened?"

Dad again.

She remembered seeing an accident on the side of the road, a truck in the river. Maybe that was a different accident.

"You were in a car accident."

Her father spoke clearly and with confidence.

Then she remembered. Their accident after the truck accident.

"Stasia?" Ellie tried to say. Her father was there beside her, sitting on a chair. He leaned in close to hear her. "Where's Stasia?" she tried to force out.

"She's asking about Stasia," her father said, turning away from her.

Mom burst into more tears and hurried from the room.

Megan shook her head toward Dad. "Not yet. Wait till she's better," she said softly without coming closer.

But Ellie realized she already knew. That night had been with her, playing over and over in some corner of her brain. Ellie hadn't been able to get out of the car. Her legs were trapped, but she wasn't in pain. It was all so surreal, the world was messed up, and yet she knew they'd been in an accident, they had to get out of the car, and they had to get some help. Her head was throbbing, or maybe her eye. She tried looking around and calling for Stasia. And then she saw her, right beside her and yet hardly visible. The front of the car had smashed into the driver's seat. Stasia was pushed partway to the back. Ellie tried to reach for her hand. She could see a little ring on her pinkie finger. Ellie called to her. Stasia wouldn't answer her. Stasia wasn't moving.

Stasia was dead. She was dead beside her before the fire began.

Fire. There had been a fire in the car.

Now it was making sense. Now she understood her mother's continued crying. And Ellie wondered why they hadn't just let her die.

Chapter 8

THE OUTSIDER
The Anonymous Blog about Life at West Redding High
November 10

I almost shut down the blog after Stasia Fuller and Ellie Summerfield were in the accident that took Stasia's life. It is still unknown what exactly happened, though despite rumors, neither of them was intoxicated. That is a fact. Why Ellie was with Stasia instead of with Ryan has inspired the wildest rumors. The truth: Ryan had been drinking, and Ellie didn't want to ride with him. They had an argument, they did not break up. It wasn't Ryan's fault. It wasn't Ellie's. It wasn't Stasia's. None of them did anything wrong.

Ellie Summerfield is in guarded condition even after three weeks. The family asked that no other details be revealed at this time.

So now "The Outsider" is fighting gossip like a superhero against crime, how do you like that? We will continue to update you on Ellie's progress. A fund in memory of Stasia Fuller has been established through California North Bank. The Outsider homecoming, unlike our school's, has been canceled. Sorry, Erica.

* * *

on't let them hurt me anymore." Ellie wondered if the tears that rained through every part of her were coming out of her eyes.

She begged everyone who came close enough to hear her whisper. They told her how strong she was, how proud they were of her, how she was getting better, that she'd get to come home before long, and dozens of other empty words meant to make her stronger. Ellie let them speak until they'd listen. Then they'd see her lips move and try to hear her words, at least at first.

"Please, please, please, Ryan, don't let them do this to me anymore."

"Dad, help me."

"Mom, they're hurting me."

Pastor Franklin, P Frank to the youth at church, was praying when she woke to pain. Her mind screamed with it.

"Why won't God help me?" she said hoarsely. And where had God gone from her? Ellie tried to go deep inside of herself, to that place safe from the searing pain.

A memory came. Grandfather Edward had shouted at her, shaking her by the arms, and she wanted to run away. The gate was locked, so she ran into the house and hid beneath the piano bench. Burying her head in her arms, she cried till the carpet was wet and her cheeks burned from the salt. *Jesus, I want my mom and dad*, she'd prayed. Before long, Dad was there. He woke her from beneath the bench and carried her to the car. Ellie knew Jesus had heard her prayer. That Jesus was good, and Grandfather was bad. But

now Jesus seemed as dead as her grandfather. He wasn't
helping her now.

And no one was saving her. They said that the doctors
had to do it, take her to the torture room and pull away her
skin, to make her heal, to make her ready to go home.

"Just let me go, please. It's too painful," Ellie said to
anyone.

"You're so strong. You've always been so strong."

"I've never been strong." And she knew that was the real
truth.

"Yes, remember when . . ."

And whoever was there with her would tell some story
from her past.

"Please let me die. Please, God, why won't You let me
die?"

And then her eyes would close and it seemed only a
moment and they'd be at her again. The little razors, sizzling
with fire, digging into her, always on one side: her face, her
neck, her arm and stomach and leg. One half had been
burned, then; that's what had happened. She was a monster
on one side.

Ellie heard a gurney wheel up beside her bed. She saw a
yellow balloon floating around the room. A window was
open, and she feared the balloon would be lost outside. An
old man lay on the gurney, and Ellie knew him. He turned
toward her and glared. Grandfather Edward sat up in his
hospital bed.

"You did this," he said.

And they were standing in a garden. The flowers by the
house had been ripped from the earth all along the neat

border. Dark, upturned earth and toppled petals littered the ground.

"What did I tell you about letting Humphrey into the backyard? Everything is ruined."

"You didn't tell me anything," she cried.

"What are you, stupid?"

She ran in her hospital gown and hid between the couch and the chair. After a time, she heard a television and peered out to see Megan watching TV with their grandfather.

"We have Twinkies," Megan said, holding one out to her.

"If she wants to stay there, let her. If someone wants to act like an injured dog, then that's what they'll always be."

And then Ellie was sinking. Her hand reached up toward wakefulness, but she couldn't reach it. Images came, the huge brown eyes of a deer, the sound of Ryan's song on her phone with darkness all around, the scent of something burning— was it her or was it Stasia?

"Ellie!" someone shouted to her. And there were masked faces all around, peering down at her, wheeling her somewhere, tearing at her flesh again, sticking a needle in her neck, opening her eyes and shining a light.

"We've got to get the fever down or she isn't going to make it."

Why all the work and effort for a life in ruin?

Dad's reading voice came through the fog. It had been there awhile, she realized. She knew the words he read. The words were grace to her, peace within the pain. She could smile from inside and imagine such a place.

"'Everyone was cheerful as the *Dawn Treader* sailed from

Dragon Island. They had fair wind as soon as they were out of the bay and came early the next morning to the unknown land which some of them had seen when flying over the mountains while Eustace was still a dragon.'"

Dad cleared his throat and paused.

"Read more, read more," Ellie said quietly as she and Megan used to say when they were kids.

Dad leaned in closer. "Well, what do you know? I thought I was reading to myself."

"You haven't read Narnia in a long time."

"I had a hard time picking which book to read from."

"I'm glad you chose that one. I've always wanted to sail on the *Dawn Treader*." Ellie glanced around the room. "Where is Grandfather? I had a dream that he died."

Dad closed the book. "He did die. He died over a month ago."

She shook her head. "He was here."

"No." Dad shook his head. "Even if he were alive, I wouldn't let him in here. But he's dead, Elspeth. He's dead."

Ellie nodded her head, but she didn't believe him.

When she woke again, there was no one there.

"Grandfather did this to me," she said aloud.

"Ellie? Did you say something?" Megan was there, sitting in the corner with a magazine. She came closer.

Ellie wondered if she should repeat it, and then decided that someone should know. "Grandfather did this. He was standing in the road. Stasia tried to miss him."

Megan remained there, but she didn't speak for a time. Then she said, "You know that he died. Before this happened."

Ellie nodded. Of course he would come back after death

to destroy her. He probably saw her wearing the bracelet. And then when she lost it, he wanted to hurt her.

"So you know he couldn't do this to you, right?"

Again she nodded. "He's dead. That's right."

But Megan didn't believe her. "Tell me what you saw."

"He was here in the hospital. And then we were in the garden. And then I was under the piano bench. And by the couch."

Again Megan didn't respond. She wasn't like their parents, so quickly dismissing what was happening to her.

"It will be okay," she said finally.

"He said I'd turn out this way, and now he's making sure of it."

A cell phone beeped. Ellie had forgotten all about things like cell phones. Cell phones and student council meetings, swim meets, football games, picnics near the dam, organized lockers, Vanessa, Tara, the guys . . .

Where was her cell phone now? All her phone numbers, and her purse? She'd forgotten about her purse. What had been in there anyway? She couldn't remember, except for her wallet. Her purse had been essential. And now she remembered nothing about it. Which purse had she taken that night? Then she thought of the bracelet. Her mother would think that Grandma's bracelet was lost in the accident, perhaps. Had anyone tried searching for her things?

"He wasn't a very nice man," Megan said slowly. She settled back down in a chair and picked up the magazine.

Ellie stayed awake for a while. The hospital sounds were muted with the door closed. Her mind was clear enough to realize that much of what she'd thought was real, wasn't. She

---

hadn't seen her grandfather in her hospital room. She hadn't gone to the garden or under the piano bench. There was no yellow balloon floating around the room, though other balloons and flowers lined a wall.

"What happened?" she whispered and barely heard her voice.

"You were in an accident," Megan said, moving to the chair beside her.

Ellie tried to nod. Yes, she knew that.

Other people had arrived. She heard Mom crying, and Uncle Henry said, "Should we go? Should I take Jane out so she doesn't scare her?"

Scare who? Ellie wondered, then realized he'd meant her. Her mother's crying might scare her. Why was her mother always crying?

"You're going to be okay," Dad said again with conviction. Too much conviction.

There was peace or at least escape in the darkness. She wanted to stay there. She wished for a heaven that was simply sleep, the deep unknowing and unfeeling place she'd found. When they forced her awake, awareness came upon her with such pain and horror.

"I need to know what's happening. How bad am I?"

But no one would answer her.

* * *

A sense of the unfamiliar pervaded the house. Megan felt as though she was visiting after years of someone else living there. She stood in the entryway with the cold November afternoon sending chills beneath her coat.

Ryan carried in her suitcase. He'd driven Megan the two hours home without much conversation. In the past few weeks, both sets of parents had insisted they come home during the week and get back to school. They'd begun sharing rides to Davis on the weekends.

"Here," Ryan said after wheeling the suitcase to the stairs. He handed her a plastic bag. "Sorry about the wrapping. But happy birthday."

Megan took the gift, trying to hide her surprise as she muttered a thank-you. "Guess I'll see you at school tomorrow."

Ryan shrugged. "I wouldn't be there if I didn't have to be."

Megan nodded.

"I better take off. You okay here?"

"Yeah." Megan was going out with James later, but first she wanted a long, hot shower to peel away the hospital scent.

Ryan left, and Megan sat on the stairs and unwrapped the bag he'd given her. She smiled. It was a book about tattoo artists and their work. How was it that Ryan could pick out something so perfect, while her own parents had given her money and apologies, and most everyone else forgot her birthday completely? She understood, of course she did. But today she thought that if Ellie hadn't been the complete center of the family before, she most certainly was now.

After Megan turned up the thermostat, she thought how her birthday would have been today, without the accident. Ellie would have brought coffee to her room and sat on the edge of her bed. Megan would groan that it was too early, but she'd take the coffee. Mom would be cooking French toast, and Megan would have made plans to meet Naomi to get her eyebrow or nose pierced—her parents couldn't stop her now. Ellie would say, "Happy birthday! Can you believe you're eighteen? You're an adult. You can vote now. I bought you something you're going to like." And despite all their differences, Ellie did always get her a gift that she liked. Maybe that was how Ryan knew to buy that book.

The first time she'd come home after being in the hospital for over a week, Megan had walked through the downstairs and then the upstairs, expecting to find the house the way she'd last seen it the night after the accident, with her parents' bed unmade, dishes in the sink, food stuck to plates. But everything had been cleaned. It smelled like someone else's house with a vanilla scent instead of her mother's favorite orange air freshener. Some ladies from the church had come, which was nice but only added to the strangeness of being home without her parents or Ellie.

As she walked upstairs, Megan remembered that first day and how she'd opened her own door to see the bed made and her clothes picked up from the floor, dresser, and bed. Neat, clean stacks rested in a laundry basket by the bed. She'd felt a rush of anger that someone had invaded her room, touched her clothes, looked at her things. She ended up sleeping in Ellie's room instead of her own.

She went to Ellie's room. She stood beside the bed and wished to see her sister with her agenda, coming back from running before anyone was out of bed, or saving the planet before 9:00 a.m.

She lay down on Ellie's bed and looked around at her sister's organized room.

Megan didn't want to be home in this empty house. She didn't want to stay at the hospital. She just wanted life to be back to normal. And yet, it would never be normal. Too much had happened, and things like eighteenth birthdays couldn't be celebrated again.

So she would celebrate with James, and maybe she'd call Naomi, Lu, Will, and the others. It was time to stop living with the cloud of death hovering all around.

Chapter 9

THE OUTSIDER
The Anonymous Blog about Life at West Redding High
December 10

Quote for the day:

> "You are good when you walk to your goal firmly and
> with bold steps.
> You are not evil when you go thither limping.
> Even those who limp go not backward."
> —*The Prophet*, Kahlil Gibran

I'd like to think that I'm going somewhere, but maybe I'm only limping forward. Thank you, Kahlil, for reminding us that even slowly forward is not backward.

That's all I've got today.

* * *

Hello, Ellie. I'm Dr. Crane. You gave everyone a pretty good scare there for a while."

Ellie could see the doctor with her right eye, but she couldn't get up or fix her hair or anything. Her left eye was swollen closed or bandaged; she wasn't sure which. Dr. Crane didn't speak to her as if she were half-dead, but as if she were sitting in his office, listening to him explain everything.

"Do you remember the accident?"

She nodded.

"Do you know that you're at the UC-Davis Burn Center?"

"I am? I thought I was in Redding," she whispered and looked around the room. "Where is Davis?"

"Near Sacramento. You were airlifted here after the accident."

All this time she'd been hours from home, and she didn't even know it.

"So do you understand the extent of your injuries?"

She shook her head.

"You have a hairline fracture to your left femur and a number of lacerations. You sustained third-degree burns on about 25 percent of your body, all contained to your left side as well. We had a scare with infection from the burn and pneumonia. You had a bad concussion as well, but you're doing well now. I'm going to explain what we've been doing to you."

"So how bad is it?"

"Not so bad. It'll take time. A lot of surgeries. But you'll have full functionality."

"What will I look like? Did my hair, is my hair . . . ?" She reached her right hand up and was surprised that it moved, then reached for her head. She found hair, though it was matted down and tangled. She tapped lightly over her head, and the pain increased.

"Your hair is still there. The burns were sustained on your left side—face, neck, arm, and hip."

"My face? How bad is my face?" Fear quickened her heartbeat. She'd known her face was injured, but the pain had been so intense Ellie hadn't worried about how her face might look or how bad it actually was.

"You've already improved dramatically."

"What does *improved dramatically* mean?" Anger grew inside of her, a type of anger she had never known. "Just tell me. And in English."

"Sweetie," Mom said, wiping away a few loose tears. "Dr. Crane is trying to tell you."

"Eventually, if all goes as well as we hope, your scars will be barely visible."

Ellie wanted to sit up. She wanted a mirror to see. "How long is *eventually*?"

"These are all things that I'll go over with you. There is dermabrasion and grafting—"

"How long?"

"It depends on how quickly you heal and how your body responds. There will be improvement every month."

"How long until the scars are *barely visible*?"

"If all goes well, that will take several years."

* * *

Megan hated school. People were nice to her suddenly. Classmates, underclassmen, and administrators said hello and tried talking to her. Her friends were nicer, and Ellie's friends acted as if she was their sister too. It was disconcerting. Wrong.

As Megan was getting some peanut M&Ms out of the vending machine, Principal Ramos stopped beside her.

"Could I talk to you in my office for a minute, Miss Summerfield?" Mrs. Ramos liked to talk to students in her office, but that usually wasn't a good thing.

Megan muttered okay and followed the principal down the hallway to her office.

"Go ahead and close the door," Mrs. Ramos said once they were inside, which also wasn't a good sign.

Megan wondered what the principal might have heard about her. Megan hadn't done anything wrong, at least not at school.

"Have a seat."

Megan sat down without saying a word.

"How are you doing through all of this?"

"All of this?" Megan said, knowing full well what she meant, but after a day of Vanessa, Lindsey, Tiffany, and others talking to her, asking if she had lip gloss and complimenting her usual black wardrobe, she wasn't in a very generous mood.

"I talked to your parents this morning, and they gave me an update on Ellie's progress. That was encouraging to hear."

Megan wondered what was all so encouraging. Her sister was alive, but in severe pain. Yeah, encouraging.

"But I wanted to check on you. You're staying at home alone."

"Yep."

"Do you need anything?"

Megan paused and then said, "Can't think of anything."

"And you are okay alone?"

She nodded, thinking that a few times she'd had friends stay over, but that didn't need to be advertised.

"And you're all right with your classes? I see that you've

kept up your grades." Mrs. Ramos glanced at the computer as she said that, obviously looking at Megan's file.

"I'm doing fine." She nodded her head.

"What are your plans for next year, Megan?"

Megan wanted to say she might go to tattoo university or volunteer for risky clinical drug trials for the pay and fun of it, but dang if Mrs. Ramos wasn't being too nice for Megan to be that mean.

"I haven't decided yet. And most likely with the hospital bills, my parents' careers, and my mediocre grades, I'll be at community college for the first two years anyway—not that there's anything wrong with community college." She couldn't help a bit of sarcasm at the end.

"That's exactly right. You can get a great education there; then you go on to a bigger school to finish out your degree."

"Exactly," Megan said as if really engaged. She looked at her black nail polish that was nearly rubbed off.

"I'd love you to be more involved during your last semester of senior year. We have a sophomore who is doing some fund-raising and updates about your sister that you might be interested in helping out with."

Megan looked at her quizzically. "I'm not Ellie."

Was that it? Was the lack of Ellie making everyone draw nearer to her as Ellie's sister?

Mrs. Ramos appeared thrown off. "I know you aren't Ellie. We aren't trying to replace her, and we hope she'll be back in school by the time we return from winter break."

"I'm sure you do hope that."

"We miss your sister; there's no doubt about it. But you're a student here as well."

Thank you, Mrs. Ramos, I didn't know I was a student here. Adults could be so dumb sometimes.

"I just want you to know that I care, and I'm here if you need me."

Megan said good-bye and hurried out, nearly running into Will, who apparently had followed her into the office.

"What do you want?" she said in her most irritated, leave-me-the-heck-alone voice.

"I sent you a text last night." Will's voice didn't disguise his annoyance.

"Do you have any idea how many people text me now? It's ridiculous. I may change my number. And you know what? I wasn't in the mood to respond. Perhaps I should put up an hourly bulletin of Ellie's progress. Host a radio show."

"Calm down. Jealousy does not become you."

Megan gave him the death stare as her hands started to shake. She knew that was what people thought. They believed her jealousy over Ellie was what incited her rebellious attitude. But part of it was simply their stupidity.

"Sorry, okay?" Will said. "I know you aren't jealous. I just want to know how she's doing." He looked genuinely worried. "Let's ditch the rest of the day and talk over coffee."

Megan glanced back at the office. Principal Ramos couldn't get too mad at her. After all, she was going through so much.

"Okay, let's go."

* * *

"I don't want to see them," Ellie said.

Vanessa, Bly, Tank, Kevin, several other friends, and Mrs. Ramos were just outside the curtain. They'd brought balloons and flowers, and they wanted to see her. They wanted to see the damage. Then they'd leave and share in shock at how horrifying she looked.

"But, sweetie, they're your friends, and your principal. They drove all the way down. They were here off and on all these many weeks. This place was packed with your friends and teachers the first few days. You should have seen it."

"Hey, Els!" came a guy's voice. "We miss you, girl. We're so glad you're doing better." And the curtain began to open.

Ellie threw up her arms. "No!"

Mom jumped up quickly and with her usual politeness asked the group behind the curtain to wait a few minutes. Maybe they'd like to wait in the hall?

"I don't want to see them. I don't want to see anyone." Ellie knew she was making it worse. None of them had ever seen her lose it. And she was losing it. "Go away!" she yelled and heard their whispers and shuffling of feet. Panic gripped her chest; she couldn't breathe. A machine started beeping, and Mom grabbed the call button for help.

"Perhaps it's too soon for visitors," the nurse said to Mom.

Ellie was grateful for the support. Mom had tried convincing her, telling her how they didn't care what she looked like. It was always about being hospitable and making everyone else comfortable to Mom.

"They wanted to cheer her up," came Mom's pathetic response.

"And did they?" The nurse said nothing else as she adjusted the gauge on Ellie's finger that measured her oxygen saturation.

"Mom, I don't want you to let anyone in here."

"But, sweetie—"

"No one but you, Dad, and Megan."

"What about P Frank?"

"I guess him too."

"And Ryan? He's already been here a number of times."

"No, not Ryan."

"He'll be so hurt. He—"

Here it was, coming again, and the anxiety rose in her chest. "I said no!"

* * *

The hospital chaplain came by to see Ellie once in a while. He talked about God and His plans and her life. She nodded a time or two so that he'd leave and move on to other bitter, needy patients.

The doctors and nurses did the usual horrific and painful extraction of the skin that tried to heal. If they left that on, she'd be scarred beyond repair for life. By peeling off the healing skin and reopening the wounds, there was hope that one day her scars wouldn't be so pronounced.

Ellie didn't want to see herself. She tried to assess the damage and the healing by the expressions of the nurses and doctors, and by her family when they saw her. Megan had to go back to school and Dad back to teaching. The holidays and school break were over, though Ellie hadn't been fully aware that it was a holiday. She mostly ignored Christmas and New Year's, as they were just bitter reminders of her confinement, her pain, and the life she no longer had. She only thought of her injuries, of Stasia and the accident. What did she look like now? What did Stasia look like now? The horror of that thought gave her nightmares.

"Ready?" Dr. Crane asked one afternoon after she'd returned from physical therapy torture. Walking had been the first step, but now they pushed her to do anything and everything that was past the limit of her pain threshold.

"I don't know." Ellie rested her fingers close to her skin, or to where her skin should be.

"You don't want to hear this, I know. But there's a lot to be grateful for."

Ellie liked that he talked to her straight. It did bother her how others had said she should be happy to be alive, reminding her of Stasia and her family. But Dr. Crane could make such statements without offense because he understood. He'd seen enough to speak it as truth.

"Other than the obvious, that you might have lost your life, you can be thankful that you aren't blind in the left eye and you have no permanent handicap from the accident. Your scalp wasn't damaged to the extent that your hair won't grow back; in fact, it's already started. You do have scars from the burns; there's no doubt about that. You'd be leading your school rallies by now if not for the fire."

Ellie gave him a frown. School rallies sounded so far, far away, nearly like some childhood memory. The past months of pain were like a progression of years.

Dr. Crane reached for her hand and led her toward the mirror.

On the right, she looked exactly as she'd always looked.

Thinner in the face, perhaps—a cheekbone more pronounced, but nothing of great significance. Then as she turned slowly, her heart missed a beat. She gasped.

"You can see the worst damage in these areas." He pointed to her shoulder, where the gown sagged.

She'd seen the damage along the outside of her arm, but not how it moved from her neck up into what had been her cheek. The skin was gone, replaced by a raw, red, melted something.

And her face. The contrast of one side to the other was shocking.

Dr. Crane talked in a clinical tone as if he were explaining an autopsy. And in a way, she was a life cut open and a life ended. "The swelling in your face has decreased immensely."

Ellie remembered when she couldn't open her eyes. She thought they were damaged, that perhaps she was going blind. But the nurse told her it was swelling from the accident, and after a few days her eyesight was fine. The pain was with her as a constant ache, and movement sent jabs of pain through her body. But Ellie had secretly hoped that her face wasn't all that bad.

"Okay, that's enough," she said, turning away.

Dr. Crane nodded. "I want you to remember that in terms of how your injuries appear, it is severe. But you are healing very well. I couldn't be more pleased. We can start the first skin grafts in a few months."

"What exactly happens with the skin grafts? You take some of my skin?"

"Yes, the best grafting is from your own skin. At times, we use donors or even animal skin."

"I'd rather use my own," and she thought of making a joke that she could be part animal or something lame like that. But those jokes never turned out well.

"Ellie. You're still a very beautiful girl."

She laughed bitterly and limped back toward the bed. "Just call me Jekyll and Hyde."

Chapter 10

THE OUTSIDER

The Anonymous Blog about Life at West Redding High

January 15

The brief popularity of "The Outsider" was lost with the lack of recent posts. Such is the way of such things, and a blog called "The Outsider" should beware of too much attention anyway. The new Web sites and blogs for and about Stasia Fuller and Ellie Summerfield keep us informed on what happened and how Ellie is healing—though be careful of believing much of anything those blogs tell you.

This wasn't meant to be a gossip column or an attempt to level the playing field between the Ins and Outs. It was simply a place to talk about the experience of someone who isn't as visible in the high school experience, and perhaps to vent a little too.

Now that we're in the new year, I've decided to stop writing "The Outsider." It was an interesting experience.

* * *

Ellie woke and saw her sister reading in the chair beside her. A stinging pain rang through her entire left side: face, neck, shoulder, arm, hand, hip, thigh, foot. She couldn't decipher which part hurt the worst. Her hand patted the bed and found the medication switch, then pushed the button over and over again. Within seconds, the pain began to ease, though it persisted like a hundred bees continuing to sting her.

Suddenly Ellie wanted to yell or throw something at Megan. How could someone sit and read with pain tearing through the room with such vengeance?

Turning her head, she saw light along the edge of the curtains. So it was daytime—late afternoon, she guessed. A small, shiny tiara rested on the bedside table, turned toward her.

"That's for you," Megan said.

"Why?" Ellie's voice was laced with annoyance.

"You won Winter Homecoming Queen," Megan said with no emotion.

Ellie groaned and closed her eyes.

"A girl came by the house yesterday to tell Mom and Dad. Mom brought it—she thought it would spur you on to recovery." Megan continued staring into the pages of her book.

"I'll give my acceptance speech next week." Ellie started thinking of clever things to say. "Thank you for taking pity on me . . ."

Megan glanced at her, then back to her book.

Ellie sat up slowly in bed. "What are you reading?"

"Tolstoy," Megan said, raising the cover of a romance novel—a woman with breasts bulging at the top of her dress, a man raising the woman's chin seductively.

"Nice," Ellie said and realized she wasn't in as much pain now. The drip was actually doing its job for once.

"The lending library here is extensive in one genre and one genre only. But this is pretty educational."

"I'm sure. So you have babysitting duty?"

"Yeah. Mom isn't sleeping well, so Dad took her to the hotel for a while with some happy sleeping pills the doctor prescribed."

"We'll all be addicted to something by the end of this."

"That doesn't sound so bad." Megan closed the book. "So they're moving you back home, I heard."

"Yeah, in a few days. Bet you're sick of the drive."

Megan shrugged her shoulders. "Ryan wants to see you. He's been a wreck."

Ellie closed her eyes. "I don't want to see him."

"He was here a few times."

She remembered that. Remembered telling him not to forget about the organ music, and how he'd cried. Ellie turned her face away and felt the jab of pain in her neck, up through her face. "I lost Grandma's bracelet."

"Yeah. So?"

But Ellie couldn't speak. There were tears in her eyes, and she wanted to escape them, to tuck every one of them back inside of her eyes. She wanted to wipe off the scars and find smooth, flawless skin underneath. She remembered in *The Voyage of the Dawn Treader* how Aslan had cut away Eustace's dragon scales, deep down to a perfect new skin.

"I need to warn you. You've got a new fan."

Ellie wiped her eyes with her good hand. She felt a sudden wave of gratitude and love for her sister for not trying to console her or join in her grief. Megan just continued on without making a big production over it all. That she was even here beside her so often was enough.

"A fan?" Ellie asked after a few moments.

"Lisa Grosen. Sophomore class. Cheerleader, and all around annoying as heck."

"Yeah, I know her. She's in student council."

"Well, she thinks she's now ambassador to our family. She talks to Mom every few days for updates on your condition. She created a Web page on the school site about you, your recovery progress, your accomplishments, quotes from you—"

"Quotes from me? What kind of quotes?"

"Oh, people send them in. You've said the most incredible things over the years. You'll have to read it."

"Tell her to stop," Ellie said.

"Um, I did. Threatened to kick her butt. She put that on the Web site—a comment about your psycho sister."

Ellie smiled at that.

"I guess your MySpace page was so overrun that she started a Web site all about you and for you. It's very cheerful." Megan said that as if it were the worst thing on earth. "She's planning this huge event for you. Wants to line our driveway with people cheering you on. Balloons and who knows what. She'll probably have a parade organized by the time you're ready to go home."

Ellie pictured everyone who had known her in school, and how they saw her as the strong and confident one—the "she's going places" girl. They'd line her driveway and get a shocking glimpse of the crippled half-monster she'd become.

"You have to stop her. Tell Mom. No, tell Dad."

"She wants to see you in the hospital too."

"I could tell her to stop."

"That was Dad's thought. Mom's sort of taken in by the

whole thing, thinks it would raise your morale. But no, seriously, don't talk to Lisa. She'd probably tape-record the event and have it up on YouTube before the day was out. She's psycho-charity-worker."

Ellie smiled. "I think you called me that once."

"She's like fifty times you, and I'm not exaggerating."

"You never do. But I'm tired. Think the magical morphine or whatever they're giving me is kicking in."

"What should I tell Ryan?"

"What do you mean?"

"He asks me if you ask for him. I'm supposed to tell you that he loves you, which is too much information, thank you. And that he's sorry for what happened. He thinks it's his fault, you know."

That woke her up a bit, though she could feel that safe, dark place pulling her downward. "Why?"

"He should have driven you home."

Chapter 11

*E*llie was transported in an ambulance to the hospital in Redding. It was the first time she'd been in a vehicle since the accident, but they gave her additional medication for the journey, which helped her to sleep.

She hadn't thought that being in a hospital could get any worse, but because she was only seventeen, she was taken to the pediatric ward and greeted by the sound of a child crying. Her parents were happy to have her closer to home, but being closer to home worried Ellie. Her friends might try harder to see her now.

Hospitals, Ellie decided, were like their own little countries. The different divisions like ICU, ER, the cancer center, the burn unit, pediatrics, and maternity were like states or cities within that country.

There was a hospital language that everyone spoke. Like *stat* meant "to hurry or be quick"; *rounds* were when a doctor visited his hospital patients (or more accurately, whenever the doctor felt like coming over from his medical practice to check up on you). *Have we moved our bowels today?* referred to a favorite hobby of the nurses.

There were citizens of the hospital: doctors and nurses and other staff, and the patients who came for long-term care or short-term. The families were tourists who came along with their backpacks and duffel bags full of things they needed for the visit. Then there were the visitors, like rabbis, priests, and social service employees. Everyone needed passports in the form of admissions papers, staff badges, or visitor passes, and security in this country was somewhat tight. They even had an X-ray machine at the entrance, after a guy came into the ER with a gun to kill his girlfriend.

Mom and Dad became friends with the other visitors. Megan wouldn't give anyone the time of day. It took Ellie longer to get to know everyone. But with nothing to do, and only basic cable on TV, she began to take an interest in the people within her pediatric region.

Little Natty had come in with an illness no one could figure out, and complication after complication kept her there.

Room 6 held Jake, who had leukemia and wasn't expected to live another few weeks.

There was Tanner, who had bone cancer, but he came and went with his chemo treatments and surgeries.

Billy was mentally handicapped and had water on the brain. He was hooked up to machines, but would rise up and smile his all-tooth-and-gum smile when he saw her.

Jessica had been burned like Ellie. But she had been asleep in bed with her mother, who forgot to put out her cigarette. Jessica's mother was dead, and the little girl had burns over 80 percent of her body.

As Ellie walked with slow, pain-filled steps down the hallway, passing these rooms, she could find some measure of gratitude. She would mostly heal, as Dr. Crane said. No part of her body was missing or maimed. Everything worked. Her mind was clear. But the gratitude she felt was drowned out by anger—anger not only for herself, but for all of these kids who had to feel this pain and endure a broken existence.

There were other visitors. Short-timers who were "kept for observation." There was a kid who swallowed an Indiana Jones LEGO figure, a boy in a bike accident whose father yelled at nurses and acted like his son's broken leg was a major catastrophe. There were kids with bad flus, the croup, and infections—from toddlers to teens.

One afternoon, after one of Ellie's minor surgeries to the deep burn on her hip, there was a tap on her open door.

Natty's mom from Room 17 peeked inside. "Natasha was hoping to visit for a bit. Do you mind?"

"That's fine." Ellie and Megan were watching TV—an episode of *CSI* they'd both already seen, but they'd found nothing else they liked.

· Mrs. Allen pushed the wheelchair, an IV bag dripping from the rolling metal stand. Natty smiled when she saw them, the kind of admiring grin seven-year-olds have for teenagers.

"How are you?" Megan asked.

"I get to go home soon!" Natty said with a happy glance up to her mom.

"Maybe by the end of next week. She's really improving."

"I can't wait." Natty's face was sickly white, and her brown eyes looked too large for her small head. Her hair was gone except for a soft brown fuzz.

Natty looked like an alien in a way, though Ellie felt bad even thinking it. She'd seen a picture of the little girl with thick, curly hair—a school photo with her frozen but pretty smile, a purple background, and Natty wearing a ribbon in her hair that matched her polka-dot shirt.

Ellie smiled at her. "I bet you can't. How long has it been?"

"Four months and almost one week," Mrs. Allen said with a sigh as she bent down and pulled Natty's socks farther up her ankles.

"We haven't been home in so long," Natty said with an exaggerated sigh. "We live in the mountains. There's a huge eagle's nest in the top of this tree that I can see from my window. Dad said he's seen two birds in it, so maybe there will be babies soon."

"I bet there will be." Megan pulled out her box of art supplies and set it on the small table. "Do you want to draw with me?"

Ellie raised an eyebrow. She'd never seen her sister be this nice to anyone.

"Sure!" Natty looked up at Megan as if her sister were the best person on the planet. "You're so pretty, Megan. I wish I looked like you."

Ellie's hand automatically went to the left side of her face.

"I'm going to draw a picture of you and Ellie."

Even at age seven, Natty was polite enough not to draw one part of Ellie's face as it really looked. The finished drawing was of two big girls and one little. They all had hair and smiles, flowers surrounded them, and a smiling sunshine dropped rays of light upon them.

The room phone rang as Natty and her mother were leaving. Megan picked it up when Ellie motioned to her. People still tried calling her from time to time, but Ellie mostly ignored them. She felt bad about it and knew she should at least write some e-mails or thank-you cards, but each day went by without her doing so.

"It's Ryan," Megan said, putting her hand over the phone.

"Say that I'm asleep."

"He's here."

Ellie shook her head vehemently.

"Here," and Megan shoved the phone onto her lap.

Ellie stared at it with her hands out, then finally picked it up. "Hello?"

"Hi." His voice was filled with concern. "They won't let me in without permission."

"Ryan. Please. I just don't want to see anyone."

"It's me, Els."

"I know. It's just . . . really, no."

She tried to give her lame reasons, but the truth was, she wasn't the same Els from a few months ago. It wasn't just her face either. She was in pain, intense pain, all the time. She didn't want to talk or hear about life in high school. She just wanted to heal and to heal alone.

"I'm coming every day until you let me see you."

And he was back the next day. Someone would tell her that he was there—the nurse, her sister or parents. He sat in the waiting room for at least an hour and then left. He did it again the next day. And the next.

"Your young man is here again," a nurse told her.

"Why doesn't he leave me *alone*?" Ellie slammed her fist onto a little origami bird that decorated her nightstand—a gift from someone, she didn't know or care whom. She smashed another and another.

Megan stood and gathered up the flat paper birds, saving several from destruction. "Just because all this happened, the world doesn't revolve around you." Megan was angry. "You thought it revolved around you before, and nothing's changed."

Ellie shook her head. "I don't think the world revolves around me. I don't want to be here. I just wish people would forget all about me."

"Well, that boyfriend of yours isn't going to forget about you."

That boyfriend of yours.

"Whatever it is you want to say to me, why not just say it? Your insults and sarcasm never worked with me before; why would they now?"

There was a flicker of a smile on Megan's face that quickly left. "I just want you to stop ignoring Ryan."

Ellie was silent for a minute, putting her hand up to her face. "I'm not ignoring him."

"He's not going to give up."

"He will eventually."

"And it's right to do this to him?"

"What am I doing to him?"

"He's your boyfriend. He's here to support you, and you won't let him see you."

Ellie thought about arguing more, going over the reasons and explaining why it wasn't her fault that he wouldn't go away. She could say that she'd write him a letter, an e-mail or text or something. But he was there, down the hall, sitting in the waiting room, again.

"Okay. Fine. Let him come in so I can tell him to go away."

Megan did smile that time and left the room. Her footsteps echoed down the corridor, and in enough time for Ellie to regret what she'd done, two sets of footsteps could be heard approaching. She tried to fix her hair into a ponytail, but the left side had been trimmed and wouldn't fit in a rubber band. Her burns were covered in a thick, shiny cream and had started to itch and burn. It was useless to think that she might look good.

There was a pause in the footsteps. Ellie could see his shoes at the door.

She didn't know what to expect when he came around the curtain. She heard him talking with Megan, a low whisper that she couldn't understand. Ryan had been there when she was barely conscious in the burn unit, but what would he do when he saw her now? What would they talk about? She determined to get rid of him quickly.

And then he was there, peeking around the curtain. Smiling the old smile. "It's about time, but I will say . . ." He walked in and pulled up a chair next to her bed. ". . . I've gotten pretty good at Scrabble by playing by myself." He set a travel Scrabble game on the bed. "Be warned."

"Uh, okay," she said.

"I also have this cool little game. It's a chess, checkers, and backgammon set in one convenient little box. Games-on-the-go." He had brought a backpack and began unloading games. Some books came next, which he set in a stack on the bedside table.

"I've also read a number of good books in the past months." He paused, but she didn't respond. "Yes, I can see you are stunned. Underestimating me as usual. I had trouble with Dickens, I will admit. But Tom Sawyer and Huck Finn just can't be beat."

She couldn't stop her smile, a smile that hurt her face and surely appeared mangled and deformed. She looked away and adjusted herself on the bed to further hide her injuries. Ryan was already setting up Scrabble.

Two hours and a number of games later, he took her hand and kissed it. Then he leaned over her and kissed her forehead.

"Did that hurt?" he asked with concern.

Ellie shook her head.

"I'll be back, then."

She didn't respond. What could she say? She wanted him back just as much as she wanted him to leave.

* * *

Megan stared at her face in the dresser mirror, with James leaning in close from behind.

"I think I'm over the piercing thing," she said, wondering why it had mattered so much in the first place. She'd been furious that her parents wouldn't let her pierce her eyebrow when she was sixteen. Then Lu had pierced hers, which infuriated Megan more—Lu was always doing what Megan wanted to do. Completely unoriginal.

"You'd look hot with a nose piercing—maybe a ring. Or one on your lip. I can't believe you don't have even one."

Grabbing James around the neck, she pulled him close, making him laugh. "You just can't believe it, huh? Because all your other girlfriends were all tatted and pierced, and you've got this pure little piercing virgin—seems you should like that."

"Well, when you put it that way, guess it is sort of cool."

He kissed her, turning her around to kiss her longer. Megan loved the way he held her elbows and leaned her against the wall.

"So, wanna get it done today?" he asked, pulling back.

She touched the gauges in his ears and wondered what they'd look like when he got old and didn't have the round wooden plugs stretching out his earlobes. Would his earlobes go back to normal?

"I don't know." There was no excitement in getting a piercing now. Perhaps because she could, or perhaps because as unique as everyone around her wanted to be, they all ended up looking like each other. The gauges in the ears, the tattoos, the piercings, the various radical hairstyles. Everything to the extreme. Everything to shock and show the anger and pain under their skin. The rebellion that ended up becoming a stereotype.

"Will you still like me if I don't do it?"

He considered a moment, then grinned. "Of course. I just thought you wanted this. And you say I never care about your life. I'd go to the hospital with you on the days I don't have rehearsal. You slam the door to your life on me, babe."

James didn't sound too broken up about it, though his words sounded good. Megan wondered if he would be as determined to be as close to her as Ryan was to Ellie, if she were the one lying in the hospital bed. But that wasn't hard to answer. No way.

"What do you want to do tonight?" he asked, sitting on the edge of the couch and pulling on his black army boots.

Megan didn't want to do anything. More and more, everything felt meaningless. The parties, the music, the anger, fights, hookups, complaining about everything . . . she just wanted to escape.

"We should go to Europe this summer," she said, leaning down to kiss James only on his bottom lip. The idea awakened her with sudden images of dark, smoky bars, funky art galleries, ancient streets and cathedrals. "Maybe Eastern Europe? Prague, or maybe Budapest, 'cause Prague is getting too touristy. Maybe Moscow?"

"The band is touring this summer. Why don't you come with us?"

She sat on the arm of the worn-out couch. "I could be your little roadie?"

He grinned. "You could be my woman."

"I thought I already was."

James paused a moment too long. "Sure. Yeah, you are."

"What does that mean?"

"It doesn't mean anything."

He shrugged, and she hated how attractive he looked with his hair a bit rumpled.

"We just never said we were exclusive. I'm willing to be that."

"I thought we'd been exclusive for a while."

He paused again, as if deciding whether to lie or tell the truth, which revealed all she needed to know. Megan looked around the floor for her shoes.

"I need to get out of here."

James swore. "Go, then."

He headed to the kitchen for a beer, and she walked to the door.

* * *

A number of surgeries were scheduled, keeping Ellie in the hospital to protect against infection. Her leg wasn't healing as they'd hoped. Ellie tuned it out, letting her parents nod in concern and write down notes about her prognosis. The old Ellie would've been on top of everything, searching the Internet for natural treatments and surgical procedures. Now she avoided it all. Mom had brought her laptop, but all Ellie used it for was to play Spider Solitaire and to listen to music. She avoided the social networks and her e-mail.

Ryan brought flowers every Sunday and Wednesday, and came almost daily for at least an hour. Sometimes on Saturdays he'd surprise her and watch TV with her all day long. Ellie felt guilty every time he came, and lonely every time he left. He was wasting his life on her. Wasting senior year.

Ryan didn't know what was really beneath the thick creams and bright-red scabs. He didn't know the half-monster of a girlfriend he had, or that she'd be this way for a long time, perhaps forever. She may never have full strength in her left leg or left arm. And the scars would be there. Already she noticed that he couldn't look her in the face for long.

Ryan was football, wakeboarding, snowboarding, hiking. He was like the sky and mountains and energy. He loved *That '70s Show*, with Kelso as his favorite character. He wanted to teach high school history and coach the same sports that he loved.

Every day that he came, she knew it was unfair not to send him away.

"I don't want you to come back here," she finally said.

He acted as if he didn't hear her. They were watching movies on his laptop. At the end of a romantic comedy, she realized once again that the two of them just wouldn't work. She didn't want him with her out of pity or guilt, though sometimes when he was there and the hours passed so quickly, she desperately wanted him to stay no matter the reason.

This will not work, she told herself. *I knew it before, and I know it now.*

But the next afternoon, he walked into the room with his backpack of fun stuff.

"Els, you have to see this new movie. It's French with subtitles. Remember how you always wanted me to get more culture in my life? Well, since your accident, I've watched *Chocolat, Moulin Rouge, Amelie, Across the Universe*, and *Sweeney Todd*—wow, that was bloody. *Moulin Rouge* was awesome. Just don't tell the guys, or I'll deny it."

"We need to talk," she said. If she did it quickly, it'd be easier.

"I'm a little worried you won't be able to read the subtitles on my laptop. Last night when I was practicing to see if I could read it aloud to you, well . . . let's just say it wasn't pretty."

"Why are you here?"

"I'm here to be your entertainment. Wanna see a magic trick?"

"No, I mean today is Monday. You should still be in basketball practice."

"We had a day off."

"They never give days off."

"Yeah, crazy, huh? Coach was sick."

Ellie didn't say more. The pain in her hip, shoulder, and neck had been nearly unbearable again. The doctor was weaning her to a lower dose of painkiller, which was easy for him and awful for her. The pain aggravated her nerves, making her easily irritated with anyone who came into her room. But she also knew the void left in the hospital room when her visitors said good-bye to her with their promises to return. Ellie wished to tell every one of them to go away and never come back—it was harder to have them leave than to never have them come at all.

Ellie closed her eyes against the pain. Ryan was setting up the computer on the bed tray. She groaned, and he jumped back.

"Are you okay?"

"I need the nurse," she muttered, and Ryan was quickly out the door.

He came racing back into the room. "She'll be here soon. Should I call someone else? What can I do?"

There was panic in his voice, and she closed her eyes again, squeezing them shut and trying to escape. Pain wrapped around her till she thought she couldn't survive it.

She must have fallen asleep, because when she opened her eyes, it was nighttime and Ryan was gone. She was too worn out to care.

* * *

"Ryan quit the basketball team," Megan said when she came by after school the next day. She set her books down on the table.

"He what? He can't." Ellie tried to sit up. Seeing Megan's books reminded her that she was getting further and further behind.

"He did."

"That's his only chance of getting a scholarship."

"He doesn't care. He might take a year off and work at his uncle's auto body shop."

"Why would he do that?"

"He wants to be near you."

Ellie sighed. The time had come. "When he gets here, I better talk to him alone."

Chapter 12

THE OUTSIDER
The Anonymous Blog about Life at West Redding High
February 2

Back by no demand whatsoever, except my own.

I'm probably writing into the air, which would be good since I'm about to insult you. Yes, YOU.

This blog began to provide the view from one senior's life who wasn't popular, a jock, or an academic. So yes, it was often a place of criticism and a bit of ridicule toward certain students. And it was fun. No one was permanently injured. However, I missed taking a hard look at the out crowd itself, which was wrong and prejudiced. I'm all about bipartisan criticism. And so I've been looking. The stoners, goths, emos, punks, gang-bangers, nerds, and whatever other groups there are out there, I just have to say—you're all stupid. I've discovered of late that people are stupid. The in crowd and the out crowd, all of you.

Not just stupid, but idiots! Myself included.

* * *

Ryan tried his usual diversion from serious conversation. Ellie reached for his hand, wishing for more strength to squeeze it harder, to make him understand that she meant it this time.

"This is a waste of time," she said. "Listen to me, please."

"Whose time? Not mine, I've got all the time in the world."

"You need to get back on the basketball team."

He sat in the chair beside her and leaned back with his hands behind his head. "Too late. I burned that bridge," he said, then cringed. "I mean, uh, I closed that door."

"It's okay to use the word *burn* in front of me."

"Yeah, I know. It's just that it sounded strange when I said it. But it's too late for basketball. I don't even like the sport that much."

"You love every sport."

"Not lately."

"Why not?"

He looked at her, then away. "It just feels meaningless or something. And I want to see you more."

She nearly laughed—or was it that she nearly wanted to cry, for both of them? "You can't even look at me."

He leaned forward, grabbing her hand. "What are you talking about?"

"You can't even stand to look at my face for more than half a second."

He shook his head over and over again. "No, it's not like that. It's not like that at all."

She had to end it. It was better for him, and it was better for her. She felt such turmoil over his coming, such guilt over wanting him here. A swift, clean break would be best. It would hurt both of them, but it needed to happen. Ryan would never end their relationship, no matter how bad it got for him. How did a guy break up with his disfigured girlfriend?

"I'm breaking up with you," she said.

"Do you know why it's hard for me to look at you?"

"I don't want you to come back here."

"It's not because of how you look."

"This will be better for you. And it'll be better for me."

"Better? How?"

Ellie closed her eyes. She hated how she was lying in a bed like a wimpy, pathetic weakling. Wasn't it obvious that he'd be better, that she was letting him off the hook?

"I can't look at you because this is my fault."

"No, it's not. So if guilt is keeping you here, listen to me. It wasn't your fault. We had that fight. I hurt you. We could go around and say that you shouldn't have been drinking that night, and I shouldn't have left with Stasia. We could say so many things. But it wasn't your fault. You didn't do this to me."

"But I should never have . . ." And Ryan broke down, his head on the edge of her bed just like when she was in the burn unit.

"It's not your fault. It isn't."

"I need you, Els."

She shook her head. "I'm the last person you need."

He stood up then, turning away from her and wiping his face with his arm. She knew this might be the last time in a long time that she saw him. Impulsively, she wanted to take everything back and to hold on to these moments with him forever.

"I wish this had happened to me instead of you," he said. "I'd do anything to take this away from you."

Ellie didn't know what to say to that at first. "Ryan. I think we hold each other back from what we're supposed to do."

A light turned on in his eyes. The realization that she didn't want him. That he was being rejected, and all the rejection she'd given him finally hit home.

Ryan carefully touched her chin, and she saw a tear stream down his strong, masculine face.

"I love you. I love you more than I've ever loved another person. I was myself with you. But you didn't take me seriously. Everyone thinks I'm just some jock, the stereotypical guy. And I played the part; there's no getting around that. Until I was with you.

"But you never let yourself really see me, or believe in me. Maybe you're too afraid to see how much I love you and to believe in it. You wanted to break up with me that night, I knew that. And I can't keep forcing you to be with me. But I'll always love you, Els. Always."

He let go of her chin, packed up, and walked out without another word.

* * *

Megan could see that her sister wanted out of the hospital. *Needed* was perhaps the more accurate word. She'd overstayed her visit. And it had become less like a place of healing and more like a prison with the confined room, bland food, visitations, and daily torture treatments.

"Who's the hot doc?" Megan asked as she pushed Ellie's

wheelchair down the hallway from PT back to her room. It annoyed Megan that Ellie had to ride like an invalid, though her sister probably couldn't walk far with her leg in pain.

Ellie shrugged. "I don't know. I don't want to know."

Megan hated having to cheer people up. She didn't do it well. "So what, you're finished with guys?" She'd seen Ryan at school earlier in the day. He looked like he hadn't slept or eaten in a week.

"Guys are the farthest thing from my mind," Ellie said. "I caught up with 'The Outsider' earlier today."

"Oh, it's back on?" Megan said as they wheeled into the elevator.

"Yeah, big surprise," Ellie said. "I'm glad you decided to keep writing it."

The elevator doors closed, and Megan stared at her sister. "You think I'm the writer of 'The Outsider'?"

"You need to push number 2," Ellie said with a slight smile.

Megan pushed the button.

Megan realized her sister wasn't just inquiring; she was convinced. What was the use of denying it? "How did you know? When did you know?"

"Um, back in September when you mentioned all the people you hated. And you called me a perky zealot." Ellie closed her eyes for a moment, which meant she was struggling with pain. The PT sessions usually aggravated something.

"You've known that long?"

Ellie nodded. "Even though you can't stand me, I am your sister."

"That's true," Megan said, and the doors opened to their

floor. They passed an old man in his hospital gown, walking down the hall with his IV cart.

"Which is true? That you can't stand me, or that I'm your sister?"

"Both," they answered at the same time, and laughed.

"Who else knows?" Megan asked, suddenly self-conscious.

"I didn't tell. If anyone else knew, then everyone would know. It'd go viral, I'm sure."

Megan thought of Ellie reading the blog and knowing who wrote it, but not telling a soul. Her sis might be cooler than she gave her credit for. "Oh, hey, sorry about the P-words and all the comments."

* * *

Ellie was going home in the morning. That was supposed to spark her interest and make her happy again.

"I have a surprise for you," Mom said before she came around the curtain.

"Great," Ellie muttered with her eyes toward the covered window.

Light leaked through the edges around the curtains, and Ellie thought about a world of light. She wanted darkness now, like a nocturnal creature or a vampire. That was it: she was like a creature of the night, and sunlight burned her skin even while she was fascinated by and lonesome for that normal world that was no longer hers. Millions of people were out there in that light, doing all the things that created life for them. No one stopped to be grateful for simply being, for the freedom to walk outside the door as the sun came up, to ride a bike, brush their teeth, hang out at a park, or go to the beach. No one thought it special to get a coffee at Cocobeans or to go to work or school every day.

"Ellie," her mom said, and Ellie realized she'd been ignoring her. How she wished to ignore everyone and just live at peace in her head now. If only her head would offer some peace.

"What, Mom?"

"P Frank is here."

"Tell him I'm sleeping."

She turned her back when he came into the room, not even pretending to sleep.

P Frank was in his midtwenties. He dressed in baggy jeans and T-shirts with a jacket, looking more like an artist or writer than an ordained minister. He'd been at their church for two years. Ellie had been a youth group leader and had gone on several short-term mission trips under his leadership.

"Your mom told me you're going home." He turned down his cell phone as he came in, which for some reason annoyed her.

Ellie nodded when he looked up at her. "Yep." She didn't want to talk to him today. If he talked about God being in control and having a plan, she thought she might throw her food tray at him.

"You know, everyone still asks about you, and we pray for you every week."

"Thanks."

"Do you want me to pray with you now?"

"Sure. Knock yourself out."

He paused at that, surprised at her bitter tone. Everyone

liked the Ellie she was before the accident. Instead of praying, he took a seat, which also annoyed her. How many people had there been, coming in and sitting in a chair beside the invalid's bed? She wished people would just leave her alone.

Ellie glanced at him. "Did you know that I had a crush on you?" She hoped that would make him uncomfortable.

"You did," he stated more than asked.

She remembered being embarrassed about liking him. He was a good-looking, single guy who not only loved God but truly tried to live a godly life—how many of those were there in the world? P Frank never hinted that there were mutual feelings, which of course made him even more attractive. Once Ellie heard one of the moms say that he'd better get himself a wife because the consistent affection of dozens of good-looking teenage girls was erosive to any man's moral fiber.

"When you first came. And again last summer." She'd been dating Ryan then, but on their trip to Mexico, her attraction to him had risen up once again.

"Yeah, I know."

She appreciated that he dropped the act. Of course he'd known. It was pretty obvious.

"Ellie, you are an amazing person."

She laughed at that. "It's okay. You don't have to let me down easy. I didn't mean it like that."

"I know. I just want you to know that I really think you're an amazing person. And I know God has a plan for your life."

"Oh, not that," she groaned. "Do you really think God is in control of our lives?"

"I do. Have you lost faith?"

"Not faith in God. Just faith in God as someone who really pays attention to the details of each life. It would be like paying attention to every ant in an anthill."

"Which isn't hard, because He's God."

"Yeah. Anyway, I don't want some deep discussion right now."

"I actually stopped by for a specific purpose. I went by your house first to bring you some mail." He pulled out a letter from his jacket pocket.

"Did I win the Clearinghouse Sweepstakes?"

"Better."

"Cool. Hand it over, then." Ellie took the envelope, hoping he'd leave.

"I asked permission to submit it a long time ago. Your mom helped."

"What?"

"The letter is from Scotts College."

"You and my mom submitted college applications for me?"

"No, we couldn't do that. It's for an overseas program. You'd have your pick of India, Africa, South America, or several countries in Eastern Europe. The doctors say you'll be healed enough to safely travel by next fall . . ."

Ellie held the envelope in her hand, staring at her name and address. Everything like before. She could just move on as if none of these months had taken place. Except, of course, for the fact that her leg pain still kept her limping and half of her face would frighten the children of whatever lucky country she chose. They'd have her seared into their memories; that was certain.

"Sounds just great." She set the envelope on the bed.

"Give it time. It might be really good for you to get out. Pray about what you should do."

Ellie nodded and let P Frank pray for her. She couldn't wait for him to leave.

Chapter 13

THE OUTSIDER
The Anonymous Blog about Life at West Redding High
February 4

Comments:
  I totally agree. People suck.
  You need some therapy, Outsider.
  Save the whales!
  This blog could make money with advertisements and affiliate marketing. www.makeamillionb4graduation.com
  This blog is depressing. I love it!

* * *

The life of the hospital went on as it always did, as it had before she'd come and would after she left. It wouldn't notice that Ellie Summerfield was gone, just as it hadn't noticed the kids who didn't leave or went out to the morgue. Such was life in the hospital, as well as life itself, Ellie thought as Dad pushed her out of the pediatric ward amid waves from the nurses, Natty, and her mother. Natty was leaving to look for her baby birds in a few days.

Ellie sank into the wheelchair seat and leaned to the left when she noticed the sideways stares as they moved through the main hospital population. *Look at that poor girl*, she imagined they thought. *What a shame.*

Ellie could walk fine. The wheelchair only made her appear further disabled, but this was hospital policy. Megan followed, pushing a cart with Ellie's belongings and the last of Ryan's flowers.

"Just a stop at the pharmacy for your long list of medicines, and we're out of here," Mom said cheerily.

Another woman waited in her wheelchair near the counter with a baby in her arms. A man, who Ellie presumed was the woman's husband, stood at the window and talked to the pharmacist at the cash register.

The mother stared down at the pink-colored bundle in her arms, adjusting the little hat with an expression of utter contentment.

Then she noticed Ellie. Her eyes leaped up to Mom and Dad, then down to her child. She smiled slightly, trying to recover.

"Oh, a little one," Mom said in her quick, nervous tone. "How old is she?"

"Two days," the woman said proudly, glancing at Ellie again.

The husband turned to his wife, holding up the little bag with a smile. When he saw them—or rather, when he saw Ellie—his expression faltered too.

From the pharmacy to the entrance of the hospital, Ellie wanted to hide beneath a blanket. She tried to pretend she didn't notice the stares and curiosity that caused people to look her way.

Mom talked incessantly. "Say good-bye to the hospital.

No more hospital for us. No more cafeteria food or hard hospital chairs."

Ellie wanted to remind her that they'd be back not just once, but a number of times for all the surgeries that waited ahead.

"I'll go get the car," Dad said, giving her good shoulder a squeeze before he hurried ahead.

Megan pushed the wheelchair now, while Mom pushed the cart. They reached the lobby, where a surprising number of people were coming and going. Ellie kept her eyes ahead.

A little girl holding her mom's hand looked at Ellie. Her mouth dropped, and she tugged on her mother's sleeve. "Mommy! What's wrong with that lady? She looks like a monster."

Megan pushed the chair faster. Mom said, "Slow down. I can't go that fast."

"Let's wait for Dad outside."

Ellie breathed in the first real fresh air she'd had in months. But she couldn't enjoy it or the evening rain turning the air fresh and new, not with cars driving up and people walking in and out of the automatic doors. Her heart was racing, and she couldn't get a full breath into her lungs. She wanted to slink down into the chair or race back to her room, to the curtains on her window and the curtain around her bed. The world was too expansive, too busy, too full of people.

Dad drove up. Ellie stood and walked toward the car as quickly as she could. As she got inside, unexpectedly her heart raced even faster. The gentle engine and feel of the seat reminded her of Stasia's car. Leaning her head toward her knees, she tried to breathe.

Calm down, Ellie. Slow down. Don't hyperventilate.

Mom closed the door, locking her inside. "You're going home!" she said.

Megan was looking at her, shaking her head. "You okay?" she asked from beside Ellie, a vase of flowers in her hand.

Ellie couldn't respond. If she did, she might start screaming or crying. Megan helped her get her seat belt on; then no one spoke as they drove away. Even Mom finally understood.

Thankfully, there were no balloons, banners, or classmates lining her driveway. Perhaps the rain had kept them home, or else someone had finally put a stop to the horrid plans. Home was so familiar and yet so strangely far away, as if she'd gone off to college for several years and was returning for the first time. She had changed. It had not.

Dad held the umbrella. Megan raced into the rain to open the front door.

"We'll get the rest later," Dad said as they hurried inside.

Ellie was glad for the rain. The sunshine she once loved felt harsh now, too bright, too hot, like a spotlight revealing all her mutilated places. She wished to live in the darkness now, where her scars weren't so noticeable. Perhaps people who gravitated toward darkness, toward the black clothing and makeup, were all about hiding something—pain, insecurities, fears, trauma. A half-burned face.

Ellie entered the front door and stopped in the entryway.

"Welcome home!" Mom and Dad said in unison, and Ellie noticed the banner hanging across the stairwell. Megan said it, too, then disappeared toward the kitchen.

The stairs stretched upward. The living room went off to the right, the kitchen and dining room to the left. She'd always thought her house was cozy, even if she wanted to modernize her mom's traditional décor that included Thomas Kinkade pictures and silk flowers.

"You guys changed it around," she stated, looking into the living room.

"Yeah, remember the TV broke last month," Mom said, but Ellie didn't remember because she hadn't been there. "We changed the furniture around when we got the flat screen and the new entertainment console."

Ellie hated the change. The coming home was hollow and cold. She wondered where Ryan was, and whether he knew she'd been released. That she thought of him surprised her. She wanted him here, jumping out from behind the couch, ignoring the fact that she was ignoring him. He'd stopped calling after a few final attempts. And though Ellie had stared at the hospital phone, wishing it would ring, and had started a number of e-mails, in the end she knew it was better this way.

"I'll go up to my room," she said.

"So you don't want anyone to come over?" Mom asked for the umpteenth time.

Ellie hesitated. She did want people over, but she didn't want them to see her. They'd act as if she looked fine, and they'd talk about school and things she wasn't a part of now. "Maybe later. I'm tired."

Mom seemed reluctant to have her go so quickly. "How are you doing on your homework?"

Ellie shrugged, taking a few steps up the stairs. "So-so."

"You'll need to work really hard, Ellie. Graduation is just around the corner."

Ellie nodded. Maybe by graduation she'd have a big square of skin from her butt stuck on her cheek. She could give a speech about it. She decided not to tell Mom this, as she wouldn't find the humor in it.

"I'll get dinner started. Bet you can't wait for a home-cooked meal."

Mom's voice, super sweet and eternally optimistic, was grating on her nerves. Ellie felt that strange new flood of anger in her chest, growing till she feared it would erupt. She needed to get away before she hurt Mom's feelings. But seriously, with everything going on, her mother thought a home-cooked meal would make everything better?

"I want to see my room, 'k?"

"Oh yes, of course, honey. Take a water bottle with you, though. You've got to drink that water. Hydration will help you heal faster. Drink, drink, drink."

Ellie hurried up the stairs.

Her room wasn't exactly as she remembered. Someone had cleaned after the aunts had left and put things in different places. Her mail was stacked on her desk, and the lamp had been moved to the left side instead of the right. Her pillows weren't in flat rectangular stacks, but standing up against the headboard. Someone had plugged in the soft white lights that wove around her bed and crisscrossed along her ceiling. Balloons, gifts, and flowers collected from the many weeks she'd been in the hospital now decorated the windowsill, her bedside table, and the back of her desk.

The room suddenly looked too . . . too something. She'd decorated in a French design with a mix of antique-looking furniture—a black wrought-iron headboard and carved wooden vanity. Square paper lanterns dangled from the ceiling, and the white lights circled the room.

Organized in a black file shelf on her antique desk were brochures for colleges, Amnesty International, and several missionary organizations. She picked up one showing old brick buildings and a smiling coed on the front.

They were the marketing materials of a different Ellie. What would she do now? She was far behind in school, though her home teacher said it was possible to catch up. But college held nothing of the charm it had so long had for her. Before long, she'd probably have brochures and literature coming for disabled adults, burn victims, support groups, and programs for the weak and pathetic.

She walked over to her giant board of photographs. Friends, school and church events, family. And herself. Herself with both sides of her face. One picture someone had given her showed her looking off somewhere. Ellie stared at her left side. That side of her face was gone forever. Sure, they would try skin grafts and reconstructive surgery. But the nerve damage made her unable to smile quite as big as before. And the skin in the picture was gone now. It had charred or blistered off. Or the doctors had scraped it off, and now that side of her was decomposing in some medical garbage can.

In the pictures, her smile was wide and beautiful. Her face completely innocent. Ellie wanted to warn that girl of all that was coming. She wanted to say, "You better prepare yourself. Your life is about to be destroyed. All that you've worked for is for nothing. Get ready."

There were no pictures of Stasia. How strange to think of that now. The girl who died beside her, whom Ellie had known most of her life and yet didn't know at all. All those years of being in class together or riding in a bus on a school field trip, playing on the same playground together or apart. How strange to think that the day would come, and now had passed, when Ellie would share the last moments of Stasia's life.

In all her photographs, there was no evidence anywhere that the night of the accident was looming in her future.

Ellie wished she could talk to Stasia, ask if she'd been pain-free during the accident, like Ellie had been. If Stasia had survived, they could've become best friends. No one else could understand how she felt. No one else had been there.

A wrapped box sat on the desk. She hadn't noticed it till now. She opened it to find an iPhone and charger, a version newer than the one she'd had. It was empty of contact information—another thing lost in the accident. But already she had voice mail and text messages in her in-box. She set the phone back down.

Someone had brought her laptop back from the hospital and returned it to her desk. The stuffed animals in the window seat stared at her like she was a stranger.

Ellie was actually relieved to escape when Mom called up the stairs, "Dinner's ready."

At the table, Megan looked annoyed. Mom was elated, and Dad appeared to be at great peace.

"This is such a blessing," he said, and Ellie knew that for them it certainly was.

"We're going to have dinner at the dining room table regularly now," Mom said, carrying in her large cast-iron pot.

"Great," Megan said in a dry tone that made Ellie smile.

Ellie took a bite of Mom's stew and stared into the bowl. It was delicious. She ate the corn bread drizzled with extra butter and honey. It had been a long time since she'd eaten anything but hospital food. She wanted to compliment Mom and knew she should, but somehow she couldn't.

Everyone in the house appeared relieved to have her home, especially Mittens, who purred and rubbed back and forth against her legs. It surely was a relief for her parents and Megan not to commute down to Davis or even back and forth to the hospital in Redding. Their lives could go back to normal now. Mom could look happily at her daughters and husband at the dining room table—where they usually only ate on special occasions. Megan could shake her head at Dad's ridiculous jokes and eat her food quickly before heading to her dark bedroom to listen to her dark music and act all dark and gloomy again. Dad could lean back in satisfaction and pat his stomach, knowing they'd come through hell and now were healing.

They were healing, at least.

"Healing happens when you take care of yourself physically and mentally," Mom was saying.

Mom went over the schedule for the week ahead. PT appointments, doctor appointments, counseling appointment. "And it'll be great to have us all in church together on Sunday," she finished with satisfaction.

Ellie shook her head slightly but decided not to say it yet. No way was she going to church. The closest she might come was to watch the service online, since they taped it every week and made the video and podcast available. But she wouldn't trouble Mom right now.

Somewhere everyone she knew was doing their own thing, living their own lives. None of them had to experience what she had been through. And she felt hatred for every one of them because of it.

Then Ellie thought of Stasia's family. Perhaps there was one family who could really understand.

* ✳ *

Megan looked at the calendar on her computer and groaned. Two and a half months till graduation. It couldn't come soon enough. Turning off her music, she stared at her door, wondering what Ellie was doing in her room.

Their parents were worried about Ellie's grades. Megan had only laughed about it at the time, telling them that her sister would be back to herself soon enough. She'd do some last-minute miracle to retain a 4.0 GPA.

But Ellie wasn't bouncing back. She wasn't the same, and Megan didn't know that being home would change that. Hopping off her bed, she went to Ellie's room, knocked, and peered inside. Her sister was sitting awkwardly at her desk chair, staring out the window.

"Let's go to TJ's and get a milkshake."

"I'm tired." She didn't look Megan's way.

From the back, Ellie looked mostly the same as always. Her long brown hair looked decent enough, not quite as shiny and not styled. But it was wavy and nice. Even the hair on the injured side didn't look bad. It was that one side of her body that was shocking. It sent a shiver of pain down people's spines to see the damage. And the stark difference from a beautiful face to the burned face was stunning.

"You aren't tired." Megan put her hands on her hips. "When was the last time you went to TJ's? Just think about a burger, tater tots, and a shake. Strawberry for you, vanilla for me."

"I don't want to."

"Come on, El. You need out sometimes. We'll take Mom's car so no one will recognize us. If I see someone, I'll speed off before we're spotted."

"You aren't going to leave me alone until I say yes, are you?"

"Nope."

* * *

Megan was surprised when Ellie ordered a peanut-butter-and-chocolate shake. Her own vanilla shake was thick and had the perfect subtle flavor. They tasted each other's and decided to share both.

"I don't think I've ever had a better shake than these," Ellie said as she sucked on the straw.

They sat silently enjoying their milkshakes in the drive-up area of TJ's. Megan had parked in the farthest stall. She almost choked on a chocolate chunk when her phone beeped.

She read the text and sighed.

"Who is it?" Ellie asked.

Megan bit her lip. She was tired of being the go-between. And she'd partly come here to talk about two subjects with her sister: graduation and Ryan. But now that they were here, confronting those issues wasn't as easy as she thought. "Will wants to see you," she said.

"Will Stefanos?" Ellie shook her head and swore.

Megan's head snapped around. Her sister actually used profanity? Megan didn't like it. And she didn't like that she'd just used the word *profanity,* even if it was in her own head.

Before she could say anything, Ellie said, "Tell him to get in line—rates to see the circus freak are high."

Megan typed into her phone and then started the car. Drastic times deserved drastic measures. And though it annoyed her how Will was so unlike himself when it came to Ellie, she wondered if he could help somehow.

At a red light, she leaned on the steering wheel. "Will's not trying to see you 'cause he's curious about how you look."

"Then why?"

"Why don't you ask him?"

"I don't want to ask him."

"He's at home in the living room."

"How do you know?"

She held up her phone.

"Why'd you say he could go in?"

"Because you need it. You weren't made to be this reclusive."

Ellie swore again.

"Watch your language, young lady," Megan said firmly.

They stared at each other. Megan couldn't believe she'd actually resorted to "young lady." Where had that come from?

They drove the rest of the way in silence, sipping the last of their shakes.

They found Will sitting on the couch. Mom was treating him like a long-lost relative. Ellie didn't turn his way, only headed straight for her room. She slammed the door shut. Mom would be mortified that the shining star of the family was being so rude.

* * *

Ellie thought the knock on the door would be her mother telling her why she should see Will, or maybe it was Megan again.

"What?" she said.

"I want to come in," Will said.

Ellie jumped up from her bed and went to the mirror in her bathroom. The same red, scarred face she'd seen hours earlier looked back at her. She looked like that guy from *The Dark Knight* . . . Two-Face, that was his name. She was Two-Face.

"I'm not dressed," she called and flopped down on her bed, sending a shot of pain through her shoulder.

"You look dressed," Will said as he opened the door.

"Nothing like intruding on people. What do you want?"

He stood in the doorway. Evening was falling, and she hadn't turned on her bedroom lights. The dimness of the room felt comforting, except that Will was there.

"Ellie, you're going to be okay."

She rolled onto her back to see him as anger coursed through her. "Thank you, Will. I'm glad to hear that."

"Listen," he said, walking toward her. "When I was in Brazil, this guy was shot, and I was with him. All kinds of stuff happened that was pretty bad. And I didn't think I'd get through it. But I did. You'll get through this. You'll have scars, but you'll be okay. Trust me."

For some unknown reason, Will's sincerity and urgent tone calmed her.

"So can I stay awhile?" he asked.

"It's a free country."

"So am I the first visitor?" he asked.

"No one else has had the guts to come over after I said I didn't want to see anyone." She thought of Ryan then. He'd have been here, but she'd driven him away.

"Guess I'll be known as the guy with the guts."

"So, you want to see?" And she turned suddenly, vulnerable and defiant. Why not let him see it? Get it over with instead of continuing to turn this way and that to hide what couldn't really be hidden.

"Of course."

His response surprised her. She didn't expect such honesty, and somehow it settled her nerves. He walked directly toward her and turned on her bedside light.

She hadn't really looked at him until now. His hair was a little longer, and it surprised her that he looked older—cheekbones and jaw more defined. His lips were full and his eyes so brown they looked black.

His expression hadn't changed. He studied her face, then her arm and shoulder that were exposed. She wore loose sweats and a baggy top. His eyes returned to look her in the eye.

"Okay?" she said. "You can go now."

"I heard you didn't like my birds."

"Your birds?"

"The origami birds I sent to the hospital."

It took a moment for her to remember the paper birds she'd smashed. "You sent those?"

"Yes. It's a hobby I learned as a kid."

"Megan saved a few," she said and motioned to her desk, where five of the survivors sat.

"Did you ever read a book called *Jonathan Livingston Seagull*?" Will pulled her desk chair out and sat on it backwards with his legs stretching out. He rested his arms on the back of the chair.

"No."

"You should."

Ellie sat awkwardly, then moved to the small window seat across from him. There was a haze in the glow of a streetlight. The winter had yet to pass. Usually February and March brought the first of green and surprisingly warm days within the cold and threats of snow, but not this year. It had been a long, cold winter, everyone said.

"It's my favorite book, I think."

"What's it about?"

"This seagull wants to improve his flying, though his flock is against his experiments. It's about pushing beyond the expected limits, going beyond the social norms despite the backlash, in the effort to be excellent."

Ellie raised an eyebrow. "And you think I need to rise above my limitations and do something beyond what my little seagull wings can do?"

"You have read it." He grinned widely, and she couldn't be annoyed with him.

"What about Michener's books?"

Ellie shook her head.

"Have you read *Gone with the Wind*? *The Power and the Glory*—another of my favorites. Greene was a great writer.

I'll bring *The Third Man* over sometime to watch. He wrote the book and the screenplay. Have you read any Chekhov?"

"You already cased out my bookshelf. You know what I read."

He laughed. "So I was hoping your works of literature were hidden in some cubbyhole. What's with the self-improvement collection?"

"Give me a cigarette," Ellie said, suddenly surprised by the yearning. Why was it that so many of the damaged people smoked?

"No. But I'll bring you some books tomorrow. Some of us have to go to school, so I'll be here afterwards."

And with that he hopped up from the chair, said goodbye, and was gone.

Chapter 14

THE OUTSIDER
The Anonymous Blog about Life at West Redding High
February 27

We have a new head chef at Cafeteria Redding High. I say "chef" because—I can't believe I'm writing this—the food rocks. Now, as a voice of criticism and angst, it isn't an easy thing for me to offer glowing reviews. But have you tried the teriyaki chicken or the Greek salad? Whatever powers-that-be hired the new cook should receive an award. It nearly makes me sad to be graduating.

And yes, Ellie Summerfield is back at home. According to her family, she will not be returning to school at this time. We should respect her privacy.

* * *

Mom took Ellie to her PT appointment—more torture and pain. Ellie wondered if there'd ever be one single day when she didn't feel pain. Again, shivers of fear crept over her while riding in the car, but she was thankful her left side wasn't facing out the passenger side.

"Do you want to go shopping for some new clothes?"

"No," Ellie said, though she wanted to scream, *Are you*

serious? How could you think I'd want to go to the mall like this?!

Mom appeared hurt, but Ellie didn't apologize. When they got home, Mom brought up her schoolbooks and assignment sheets, reminding her that Mr. Carr was coming on Friday to check her progress. Ellie turned on a soap opera and rested in bed. In a half hour, she figured out that some guy had come back to town after being thought dead, and wanted his wife back. The wife had married a doctor who had knocked up a patient who had gone crazy when he wouldn't leave his new wife. Ellie changed the channel, flipping through movies and talk shows and settling on a home renovation program.

A knock on the door woke her. Will walked in with an armload of books and movies.

"You know, my parents never let me have a guy in my room before."

"Maybe they don't think of me as a threat?"

"Before they would have said, 'We trust you, Ellie. But even the appearance of such a thing isn't a good idea. And temptation sneaks up on you.'"

"So are you tempted?"

She laughed at that.

"Ouch. You laugh at the idea of being tempted by me."

"That's not why I laughed."

She was flirting with him, actually flirting, with half her face disfigured and her body bandaged. She must look ridiculous.

"Will you please give me a cigarette?"

"Why?" he asked.

"Why do people normally ask for cigarettes?"

"I'm all out," he said, shrugging his shoulders.

"Guess I'll go get one from Megan's room."

"This is a bad idea." He pulled a pack out of the pocket of his loose-fitting shirt. "Your parents won't find me as non-threatening if you get caught. And I'd bet your doctors would find smoking about the last habit you need to acquire."

He tossed her a lighter. Ellie opened her window and sat beside it. She flicked the lighter on and lit the cigarette. She took a slight puff, careful not to fill her lungs too quickly, like most first-timers did. The action and the taste relaxed her.

"This isn't my first roller coaster."

"I think the correct phrase is, 'This isn't my first rodeo.'"

"Yeah, I like my roller coaster better." She inhaled again and felt it calm her nerves. She'd always thought smoking was stupid, and it was just that. But she hadn't appreciated the comfort it provided, some strange immediate relief. Mittens came to the screen and meowed, giving an odd sniff of the air, and looked at Ellie as if she was doing something wrong. Ellie ignored him. "So what's with the books and movies? Trying to educate me?"

"You may have a 4.0, but I'm discovering some real flaws in your education. We're going to start with the films of Orson Wells." He held up a DVD case.

"*Citizen Kane?*"

"You've seen it?" he said in disappointment.

"No, but I heard it's supposed to be one of the best movies ever made."

"*The* best. And with a lot of scandal attached. William Randolph Hearst, who was the media mogul of that cra, was so angered by the plot that he tried to stop the movie from being aired."

Will grabbed her cigarette, took a drag, and then carried it into the bathroom, where he flushed it.

"Hey!" she said.

"You aren't going down that road."

She shook her head, feeling a twitch of pain in her neck, and closed the window. "What was the scandal about?"

He took out the DVD and pushed it into the machine. "Let's watch; then I'll tell you."

There was a light tap on the door.

Will reached for a bottle of her perfume and gave the air a few quick sprays. "You've done enough to your parents."

"What's that supposed to mean?" she asked.

The door opened a crack. "Ellie?"

"Yeah, Mom?"

"Sweetie, I didn't know when you'd like this back." Mom held a box in her hand. "Oh, William, I didn't know you were here. Megan made some cocoa, and I bought animal cookies —the ones with pink and white frosting and little sprinkles on top. They're Ellie's favorites. I'll bring you some."

"Thanks, Mrs. Summerfield."

"So, what is that?" Ellie asked. She did hope her mother wouldn't catch the scent of cigarettes in the room.

"Oh, the box, yes," her mother said. She carried it to the bed and set it down. "It's different items recovered from the accident."

Ellie pulled back from the box as if burned. It was like a tiny coffin holding the dead. Would she find Stasia inside there, or maybe her own lost soul?

"Do you want me to bring it back later?" she asked, stuttering slightly when she looked at Ellie's face. She glanced over to Will for help in rectifying the moment, the way she always did with Ellie's father. *What do I do?* the look seemed to ask. "Stasia's mom went through and picked out what she thought belonged to Stasia . . ."

"Just leave it," Ellie said.

Mom hesitated a moment, then left muttering that she'd bring up cocoa and cookies in a while.

Will and Ellie stared at the box. Then Will rose and moved to the window, opening it wider. He pulled out his cigarettes and tapped out two, handing Ellie one when she joined him at the window.

"This is your last. You don't want to get sick. And we definitely don't want you to get hooked. Smoking is not as cool as I make it look."

She smiled at that and took the cigarette.

They didn't talk, only smoked side by side, turning slightly to blow the smoke out the window. When they were finished, Ellie took the cigarette butts and went to her bathroom and flushed them down the toilet. She caught her reflection in the mirror, the bad side, and paused to examine it in the light.

"Okay, let's see what treasures were recovered," she said, walking out of the bathroom and trying to brush away any foreboding.

The bed creaked as Will gathered the pillows behind his head and got comfortable.

Ellie paused, smiling at him. "You know that I've never been allowed to have a boy in my room before, and now you're stretched out on my bed."

"I told you, parents think I'm harmless."

"I doubt that. If anything it's because you're polite and say 'Mrs. Summerfield.' And are you harmless?"

He paused then and smiled. "Depends on what you define as harmful."

They were flirting again, and it again made her feel ridiculous.

"What's with the cloud over Sunshine's face?"

"Shut up," she said, suddenly annoyed.

"We'll talk about that soon enough," he said.

"Talk about what?"

"Your issues," he said lightly, which angered her more. He laughed. "Come on. Let's see what's in here."

She wanted to say something back, but he was looking at the box.

"You open it," she said.

"Okay." He rose from the bed.

"Wait—" She hadn't expected him to say okay.

He stared at her, waiting.

"All right, go ahead. Bring it here."

He took the box to the floor, patting the carpet for her to sit down beside him. They sat with the box between them like a treasure about to be opened.

"It's like Pandora's box," Ellie said softly.

Will nodded as he stared at it. "In the Greek myth, Pandora's box was actually a large jar. When she peered inside, she unleashed all these bad things into the world, like sickness, hardship, and toils."

"I'm supposed to be the brainy one. Didn't you nearly flunk first grade?"

"Einstein got poor grades in school as well."

She smiled. "Quite the comparison."

He nodded as if she'd agreed with him. "There is one other part to the story that is very important. Are you paying attention?"

"Yes, and avoiding opening the jar of toils and sickness. I think you'll have to open it and put the curse upon the world—not another woman who can be blamed for the sins of mankind."

"Ah, the feminist revealed." He laughed when she punched him. "Okay, so dear, curious Pandora had the gumption to—"

"Gumption?"

"Such words are necessary when discussing mythology. Now, as I was saying before your rude interruption, Pandora had the foresight to close the jar and retain one final item inside."

"What?" Ellie couldn't remember the details of the story.

"Hope."

"Hope? So hope was trapped back in the box?"

"The jar. Yeah, apparently."

"What does that mean?" Ellie suddenly didn't want to know. She didn't want a discussion about hope. "Let's just open the box—not the jar, the box."

He smiled—and it was a pretty nice smile—and motioned for her to go ahead.

Ellie pulled open the flaps. She stared at the contents inside and caught a slight scent of charcoal or fuel that made her stomach instantly sick.

She pulled a purple stuffed animal out of the box. "This isn't mine." But then she remembered holding it that night.

She hadn't known it was a cute little dog with black button eyes. Its purple fur was dirty, and the smell of smoke became stronger in her nose.

She set the dog on the floor and looked at the other items. A bottle of Victoria's Secret lotion—Vanilla Jasmine—which also wasn't hers. CDs, a book, papers, a compact, and some lipstick that she recognized.

"Only half of this stuff is mine."

"Let me see those," Will said when she pulled out a stack of CDs.

Ellie handed them to him. "My iPod was never found," she said more to herself than to him.

"Cryptonic. Owl Eyes, Krater . . ."

Will shook his head, and Ellie suddenly wanted to touch his hair, with its thick curls. She wanted to lie in bed beside him and sleep a long while.

"Who was Stasia, anyway? She looked so sweet and somewhat boring on the surface, but then you get this little view into her life, and she's pretty interesting. I would've guessed her for Pink or Justin Timberlake maybe, but not these."

"We listened to country music and classic oldies in the car before the accident."

"Really? She had a double life, then."

"Yeah, like who gave her the stuffed animal that her mom thought must be mine?" Ellie picked up the little dog once again.

"It was important enough to keep in her car, and obviously in a visible spot."

"Guess we'll never know. No one ever will."

At the bottom of the box was a book.

"My organizer," she said with surprise, almost afraid to open it. It was like opening the life she'd had that was now dead. Her left leg was aching from sitting on the floor, so she stretched it out.

"First of all, what kind of person takes her organizer to a party?"

"I grabbed my larger bag because I didn't know what we were doing that night, and I like to be prepared."

"For someone so popular, you sure have some nerd qualities."

"Nerd? Who uses the word *nerd*? And what does that make you, Mr. Greek mythology geek?"

"If the word fits, and by the way, there's no shame in being a geek. That's a far cry from nerd. Do you see any billionaire nerds—no, you do not. Do you see billionaire geeks—'most every single one."

The joke fell a little flat as they stared at the box and its contents spread out on the carpet.

"That was my life," Ellie said, opening her organizer. "What's the date today?"

"March 27."

Ellie flipped the pages. "Look, this weekend I was supposed to emcee a fashion show for a women's club. I wonder who they got to replace me."

She turned the pages back to the date of the accident.

Special date with Ryan. ☺ *Party at Mitch's.* ☹

"Stasia was still alive on all the boxes before this one. And she's dead for all the rest and forever." Ellie pictured the thousands of boxes ahead that did not include Stasia in this world. "That's my before-and-after box too."

Will nodded.

Ellie thought about that night. The night that changed everything. "I ruined our date, which made it a horrible party."

"How did you ruin it?"

"Ryan told me he loved me. I couldn't say it back. He had all these plans for us. He was upset about it, really upset. That's why he started drinking at Mitch's."

Will didn't say anything for a long time. "You didn't love him?"

She shrugged. "I don't know. I miss him. But maybe I couldn't really understand or believe that he loved me as he thought he did. It's better for him to just move on."

"What about you?"

"What about me?"

"Is it better for you to move on?"

She closed her eyes a moment. "Move on . . . what does that mean for me now?"

"What would it have meant for you then?"

Ellie thought a moment and just didn't know. The words were easy to say, but before the accident, like now, she'd been trapped in a place that all her efforts, all her accomplishments, all her drive hadn't been able to pull her from. It was like sprinting full force on a treadmill. People praised her, but she wasn't getting anywhere.

"Maybe if I could have moved away . . ." Her voice drifted off.

He kissed her then, leaning in and over the box. The taste of his mouth sent shivers throughout her body. He pulled back slightly and then kissed her again until Ellie shied away, bending her damaged side toward her shoulder. Why would he want to kiss her?

He either didn't notice her embarrassment or pretended not to. "I'm taking advantage of this friendship, you know. Is that harmful?"

She smiled then. "Maybe I'm taking advantage of it too."

A tap sounded on the door. Will rolled onto his back, and Megan came in with a tray.

"If anyone calls me Martha Stewart, I'll hit you," Megan said, though her expression faltered a moment at the sight of them. Ellie sat up. She wondered if Megan had a thing for Will, despite her words to the contrary.

"Which one of us would do something like that?" Will said.

"I see Mom gave you the box." Megan set the tray that held a plate of cookies and two steaming mugs on Ellie's desk. She pointed toward the purple dog. "You were holding that," she said.

"I was holding it when?"

"When they pulled you out. They couldn't get you to let go of it until your surgery."

"It's Stasia's," Ellie said. "I guess we should give it to her parents." The black button eyes looked at her with empty compassion.

"It's not Stasia's." Megan leaned up against the back of the desk.

"It has to be. It's not mine."

"Ryan gave it to you."

Ellie shook her head, racking her memory of that night.

The candlelit pathway for their picnic, the party at Mitch's, Ryan's drunken declarations . . .

"No, he didn't." Again the stuffed animal seemed to stare at her. Her favorite color as a child had been purple—Ryan knew that. He also knew her favorite pet—a dog named Purple, who had died of cancer the summer before. But she had no memory of his giving her this little dog.

"He said he put it in your purse as a surprise before the party."

Ellie glanced at Will, but for some reason he simply stared down at the box and fiddled with the edge of her appointment book.

"Well," Ellie said finally, setting the dog out of view. "Does anyone want to play a board game?"

Will and Megan looked at her with mixed expressions.

"A board game?" Megan asked.

"If not, then how about one of Will's movies? Some dark montage about the social ramifications of politics in post–World War II South America?" Ellie put the contents back into the box. She closed the lid quickly before she could feel bad for the little dog.

"Funny," Will said. "That would be post-Vietnam, by the way."

"I vote for Marsha Brady's board game," Megan said in mock enthusiasm.

"Who?" Ellie asked.

Megan and Will gave each other humored expressions. "*The Brady Bunch*?"

"Oh." Ellie had heard of the show but hadn't ever seen it. In her old life, she rarely watched television. "So I may not know TV trivia, but at least I'm not Martha Stewart."

Megan's mouth opened in surprise as Ellie and Will laughed.

* ＊ *

What has happened to my life? Megan wondered as she scrolled through the list of contacts in her phone. Naomi and Lu were down in the city at some belly-dance show. They were trying to convince her to join a class and had wanted her to come with them. Now Megan wished she'd gone. She looked at the text that had come through while she played board games. Board games—everyone would laugh at them for that.

> James: Babes, I want to see you. Playing at
> Cocobeans tonight. Let's make this right.

Megan wondered what could make them right. Something about James, or maybe about trouble, drew her. She was restless and grouchy otherwise.

"I'm going out," she told her parents, who sat on the couch, waiting for *Planet Earth* to come on.

"Be careful," Mom said, glancing after her with her usual worried expression.

I'd rather not, Megan thought.

* ＊ *

Ellie lay still in bed—oh, for the days of tossing and turning without pain shooting through her left side. She thought about how small her world had become. Would it always be this way? On impulse, she typed in her first text message in months.

Ellie: Hi

Vanessa: Hi? Is this really u???

Ellie: Yes. Just got a new phone. I haven't had one.

She could have had a new phone earlier, but she'd refused her parents' offer while still in the hospital.

Vanessa: I've been so worried. You wouldn't see me,
    and then you dumped Ryan. I've been going
    crazy wanting to talk to you.

Ellie: Sorry.

Vanessa: I'm trying to understand. I know I can't
    really. But I am your best friend!

She and Vanessa had said they were BFFs a hundred times. But Ellie realized how little she'd actually thought about Vanessa in the past months. She'd never shared her heart and soul with her, though they'd been friends since seventh grade. Vanessa was fun to be around. She needed Ellie's advice for just about everything in life. But Ellie didn't lean on Vanessa.

Ellie: I was in so much pain. Still am a lot of the
    time. And you know how I am.

Vanessa: Miss Independent who figures out life all
    alone and then comes out with her plan. I fig-
    ured you'd show up one day better than ever.

Yeah, like that'll happen, Ellie thought.

Her phone suddenly rang. Vanessa's number showed on the screen.

"Just don't let me hear important news about you from someone like Dwight Kellogg ever again, got it?"

Vanessa's voice sounded so familiar that it made Ellie smile and realize how much she had missed her. "Dwight Kellogg?"

"Yeah, his dad works in the hospital or something. Imagine how embarrassed I was to learn from Dwight Kellogg that my best friend was home."

"Okay, I promise not to ever let you hear something about me from Dwight Kellogg ever again."

"Aren't you funny?" Vanessa said. "Oh, oh, there's so much to tell you."

Ellie laughed, but she suddenly wanted off the phone.

"Did you hear about Jill and Tyler?"

"I haven't heard anything. But, V, I can't talk long. I'm feeling my meds kick in, which means sleepy time."

"Oh yeah, okay, sorry."

"We have a lot to catch up on." And then Ellie realized that by texting Vanessa she'd opened a door. Now Vanessa would want to see her. And so would everyone else.

"Have you talked to anyone from school?"

Ellie worked at peeling the sheet from her shoulder where it had stuck to an exposed scab. She winced as she finally tugged it free.

"Only my sister, but she doesn't say much." Ellie didn't mention Will. The fewer questions, the better.

"So you don't know?" Vanessa's tone was a mixture of seriousness at the subject and excitement that she got to share some shattering gossip.

"I'm guessing that I do not."

Vanessa paused, then said, "You broke up with Ryan, right?"

"Yeah. I guess I did."

"And did you know he's going out with someone now?"

Ellie sat up slightly. *Tara*, she thought but couldn't say.

"He and Tara are going out," Vanessa said in disgust. "I was starting to really believe in Ryan. He seemed so real about how he felt about you. And then, just like that, he's with Tara."

"It's been a month, I think," Ellie said. Her heart was racing, and it was hard to breathe for a moment. "When did they start going out?"

"Recently, I think. They were holding hands at lunch today. I couldn't believe it. I didn't know if I should tell you."

"Of course. It's fine. I mean, really."

"Well, as long as you're okay about it. But still. Tara? We knew she was after him. She probably heard you were home and decided she better not wait any longer to sink in her claws."

A sudden nausea swept over Ellie. She wondered if her meds weren't sitting well in her stomach. "I better go."

"Okay, well, I could come over tomorrow."

Ellie sighed, wishing she'd never sent the text. "Call me tomorrow. I'm getting close to another surgery, so I may not be able to have visitors. They want to protect against any viruses or infections." It was a lie, but Vanessa would believe it.

They got off the phone, and Ellie realized she was shaking.

She didn't want to see Vanessa, or any of her old friends.

She didn't want to hear about Ryan and Tara. For some reason, she couldn't get the image of them holding hands at lunch out of her head. Suddenly she wanted to throw something.

Ellie couldn't really blame him. Yet why Tara? Would someone else have been easier for her to hear about? She didn't know. Did Ryan talk about her to Tara? Did they feel sorry for her? Or was Tara gloating over finally having him?

Would he create a candlelight surprise for Tara too?

She could imagine Tara leaning against Ryan seductively, weaving her fingers through his, tossing her hair back and kissing him.

Ellie grabbed up the purple dog she'd retrieved from the box earlier and threw it across the room.

Chapter 15

THE OUTSIDER
The Anonymous Blog about Life at West Redding High
April 12

Graduation is closing in for us seniors. I for one cannot wait to move on from high school. Since there's suddenly become a witch hunt to find out who I am, I might as well reveal myself. Picture me taking a bow. Megan Summerfield, which shouldn't be a surprise.

* * *

Sighing in annoyance, Ellie shifted in the chair and stared out the window to the view across the Sacramento River. The currents moved in wavy, slow lines.

"I feel like I want to go home," she said to the woman sitting across from her.

Her counseling sessions were sort of helpful, Ellie had to admit. But sometimes she just wanted to pinch her lips closed with arms folded at her chest. Dr. Montgomery—Maggie, as she insisted upon being called—thought she knew everything, and it drove Ellie crazy.

"Why don't you tell me about Will?"

"What about him?"

"Are you attracted to him?"

She shrugged her shoulders.

"Have you talked to any of your old friends?"

"Just that one talk with Vanessa. So not really."

Maggie wrote some notes on a yellow notepad. Ellie thought she must be in her forties, and she was attractive for that age, with short dark hair and perfect makeup. But she was divorced, so how much did she really know about this counseling stuff?

"How do you feel about that?"

"Glad. I don't want to talk to them, and I'm glad they're leaving me alone. I hope that continues."

"But you're okay being around Will?"

"I guess."

"Why do you think that is?"

A fishing boat came into view with a rumble of its engine. The driver was standing with his hands on the steering wheel as two other men talked and held their ball caps to their heads. They all wore thick jackets in the chilly April afternoon.

"I don't know why. I didn't have much choice. He sort of shoved his way into my life."

"But Ryan did that as well, and you told him not to come back."

"Maybe Will and my sister are easier. They have their own broken stuff or something. Ryan was too . . . I don't know what. It just seemed like a waste of time for him to keep seeing me."

"A waste of your time or his?"

"His." Ellie remembered Will asking this same question.

Maybe her insurance company should pay him for counseling advice.

"But it's not a waste of Will's time?"

Ellie glanced at the clock. Was this therapy or an interrogation? Her parents were making her come to these sessions, and at first Ellie thought, *Why not?* But she didn't want to analyze everything. She didn't want to deal with Stasia's death or her disfigured face. Didn't want to talk endlessly about her feelings or why those feelings existed.

"Will is more like me. I can just feel it, so don't ask me why."

"Do you think it could lead to more than friendship?"

She thought of the kiss. Something they hadn't talked about in the week since it happened. "Why do people think that a boyfriend relationship is *more* than friendship? Why is that better, or more?"

"You're right. I apologize for my terminology."

Even when she was wrong, somehow Maggie turned it around toward being right. Who used words like *terminology* anyway?

"I only want friendship," Ellie said, again looking out the window. The boat had disappeared from view.

Maggie was silent, which she often was when she didn't believe Ellie. The clock on the wall ticked loudly.

"Ellie . . . do you think you are worthy of a man falling in love with you?"

Ellie's eyes darted back to Maggie, and her hand instinctively moved toward her face.

"Worthy?"

"Do you think your life has the value that it had before?"

She didn't respond. Of course it didn't. She was nothing now. Before, she was doing things for others; she was accomplishing goals; she was working hard. Now she did none of those things. Her life obviously didn't have the same value.

"Do you think your worth, your value as a human being, is connected to how you look?"

"Of course not," she said defensively.

"Of course not? Why do you feel of lesser value now than six months ago?"

"Did I say that I did?" She glanced at the clock again.

"Let's talk about this in our next session."

"Sounds fun. Perhaps we should talk about my grandfather as well."

"If you are finally ready to, then yes, absolutely."

Ellie hated when her sarcasm didn't affect Maggie.

"Before we end, I want to talk about the stages of grief."

"Wonderful. Do I get a sticker when I leave for all my pain and suffering?" She glanced down at her phone and typed to Megan:

Almost done. Come save me.

"So this is as bad as the dentist's chair?"

"I was thinking the doctor's office, and I'm getting a flu shot."

Maggie only nodded. "Here is a paper for you to take home that describes the stages of grief. However, you'll probably recognize the stages best once you're through them."

"A chart that helps after you've gone through the chart. Helpful."

"Surprising, isn't it."

Ellie took the paper from Maggie's desk and sat back down. "Stasia wasn't like this close friend of mine. I don't really feel like I'm grieving for her."

Maggie leaned back in her chair as if she'd expected this. "You're grieving many things right now, Ellie, whether you realize it or not. You've lost the life you had—a life free from the pain that you've already endured and will continue to endure. You had someone die beside you—best friend or just an acquaintance, that has a very big effect. You lost your boyfriend, the dreams and plans you had . . ."

Ellie straightened up and felt the usual groan of pain in her leg. "Wait, wait a minute. I didn't lose my boyfriend or the dreams and plans I had. What do you mean by that?" A ball of anger grew in her stomach. "What, because I'm a monster now? Is that what you're saying? I can't do any of my dreams and plans because I look like this?"

Maggie never got rattled—something else that annoyed Ellie. She wanted to shout or throw something, but Maggie would probably still sit there as calm as a Zen master.

"That's not what I said, Ellie. You were a different girl last November. And so you grieve for that girl as well."

Ellie couldn't argue, because a small part of her recognized there was truth here.

"It's similar to children of divorced parents or for anyone who has experienced trauma. There is the event and circumstances surrounding what happened—in your case, the night of the accident. But there is grieving and anger over what you lost—how you've undergone suffering, and so you aren't the same. There's also guilt involved. I had one young man who could never release the guilt he had over his parents' divorce. His father had told him about his affair, and he now believes if he'd told his mom, maybe they could have worked it out."

Ellie didn't want to hear this anymore. Instead she wondered if she knew that guy, and wished to ask his name. Did he go to her school?

"Do you understand?"

"Yes," Ellie said.

"What do you understand?"

Ellie sighed. Here was the part where she had to relay back what she'd learned. "That I'm not the only person angry in the world, and my guilt is normal, and that stuff."

Maggie appeared satisfied. They talked a short time longer, and Ellie was released with instructions on what to work on for the week ahead: studying the stages and considering what makes a person worthy.

Megan was nearly asleep in the car, with her coat zipped to her chin. She pulled the earbuds out of her ears and sat the seat back up.

"Thought you were going shopping while I was in there," Ellie said.

"I hate the mall," Megan said, turning the key to start the car. "What's that? Therapy homework?" She pointed to the paper in Ellie's hand.

"You know, you might consider some therapy yourself."

"Yeah, but then I'd lose my rage toward Mom and Dad and would have no excuse for this bad attitude I enjoy so much."

Ellie laughed at that. She had not fully appreciated her sister's humor; now Megan often made her laugh.

"These are the five stages of grief that I'm experiencing—or so Maggie says." Ellie dramatically read each stage and its accompanying description.

"1. Denial: 'This can't be happening!'

2. Anger: 'It's not fair!' 'How can everyone else just accept this?'

3. Bargaining: 'I'll do anything . . .'

4. Depression: 'What's the point?'

5. Acceptance: 'It'll be okay.'"

Even as they joked about each stage, Ellie felt her annoyance grow. What oversimplified, stereotyped drivel. She wanted to rip up the paper and throw it out the window. Maybe that meant she was in the "anger" stage. She was in all the stages at the same exact time, so didn't that eliminate their being "stages"? And how was it helpful to see such a chart?

"I want to see where it happened," Ellie said suddenly.

"What?" Megan said, but then her face registered a look of understanding. She shook her head.

"I want to see it."

"Why? And why right now?"

"Why not right now?" Ellie glanced at Megan but then kept her eyes ahead on the road. Otherwise the panic would come, as it did whenever she rode in a car.

"You just had a session. You don't seem very happy."

"I'm not happy. How could I be happy?"

"The old, optimistic you would have told the new, bitter you to have more faith, to cheer up, to believe that God has a purpose . . ."

"Just take me there, okay? Or I'll drive myself."

"You aren't supposed to drive."

"I know. So I guess you better drive me."

Megan was silent. They came to a four-way stop sign, and she sat there with the car idling.

"Turn left," Ellie said. "People are waiting."

A guy in a truck waved for her to go ahead. Still Megan sat there, even as the guy went by with his hands thrown up in frustration. Someone honked behind them.

"Will you just turn left? It's not that big of a deal. I just want to see what it looks like."

Megan put on her left turn signal. "This is a very bad idea."

"And when have you ever cared about an idea being good or bad?"

Megan shook her head. "Was I this much of a pain in the butt?"

"You still are."

* * *

Ellie would not have recognized it in the daytime. The road was northeast of Redding in an area she didn't know so well. That night of the party, she hadn't been paying attention to the road. Perhaps if she'd driven up and down that stretch, eventually she would've found the spot. Megan knew just where to pull over.

Turning off the engine, she looked at Ellie. Their eyes met, but neither spoke as they got out of the car.

There were light skid marks still on the road where Stasia had tried to miss the deer. And somewhat hidden in the late afternoon shadows, a wreath of silk flowers was nailed to a tree. The road was peaceful, with only an occasional car passing by. Beyond the trees, the foothills rolled up against the taller mountains surrounding the city. This was a stretch of country between the subdivision where Mitch's father lived and the town of Redding.

Ellie wished she'd worn her warm jacket as she began to shiver in the cold afternoon. She stared off the road where it sloped slightly. The bushes were broken, and as she walked through the damp, golden grasses, the site of the accident could be detected, but only faintly. The trees and earth were already covering it up. Green grass sprouted close to the earth, nearly hiding the indentations of where the car had come to rest and where emergency vehicles had come to surround them.

Ellie wondered what it must have looked like from the viewpoint of the people who came to help, from the first car to spot the accident to the paramedics rushing forward with their gear. She knew the inside view. Had Stasia ever been conscious after their initial impact? Both girls' blood had seeped into this very ground. This was the place where Stasia forever left the living and joined the dead.

Something caught her eye at the base of a thick, spiny bush. She reached for it. A thorn caught her sleeve, and Ellie felt the sting of its point entering her skin. Still she reached toward the object half-buried in the dirt.

She grabbed it, already knowing what it was. Once her most valued possession.

"Look," she said, holding up the cell phone for Megan to see.

"It probably doesn't work, but try it."

Ellie held down the power button, but nothing happened. Then she noticed the crack in the screen. The night of the accident, she remembered it ringing, and she'd tried to get to it. Ryan's ringtone. "Electrical Storm." The soundtrack to Stasia's death.

"What did they do with Stasia's car?"

Megan shrugged. "Probably sent it to the junkyard."

Ellie nodded absently. Everything eventually ended up in the junkyard, it seemed.

"Okay. Let's go home. I've seen enough."

Ellie didn't want to see anyone the rest of the day. She told her mom that she didn't feel well, setting off the chain reaction of thermometers and a long round of questions.

"I have cramps," she lied, which effectively ended her mother's panic and kept Will from coming up the stairs.

She kept the lights in her room low, turning on *The Motorcycle Diaries* that Will had left for her. Reading the English subtitles made her sleepy, and later she awoke in the dark with Maggie's questions sounding in her head.

But really, what was she now without her face? With a body that was always in pain? On the surface that sounded superficial, but the fact was, her looks, her strength, her drive and passion to achieve had built her confidence for as long as she could remember. What did she have without her confidence? Why was her self-confidence so tied to being able to walk with fearless strength, unconcerned with how she looked?

Why was she so afraid now?

Yes, death had come to visit. Death locked her in that car, but it had chosen Stasia and left her to live. It had taken her grandfather and eventually would take everything and everyone she loved and hated. She'd always had her faith in God. Now she felt that Death was a larger god than God Himself. *No, no,* she told herself. She didn't believe that, not really. But she knew Death's face better than God's. She felt the suffering of death in her scars and wounds, whereas she didn't feel God at all anymore.

And now with her friends mostly gone, and everything and everyone moving on without her—oh, how wrong Ryan had been when he said the school couldn't survive without her; even he was surviving well without her—what had been the point of all she had done? Food drives, spooning mashed potatoes and giving a smile to the lines of homeless at the rescue mission, student council meetings, and all her pages of plans and to-dos.

What was the point in all those things?

Grandfather told me, and now it's come true.

He had held her chin and looked her straight in the eye. Mom was in the hospital, recovering from what Ellie now knew was a hysterectomy. Grandfather picked her and Megan up from grade school. When Ellie showed him her math paper that said "100%" and "Great job!" Grandfather suddenly came unhinged.

"Who do you think you are? All Miss High and Mighty. You think you're better than everyone else."

He'd bent down to face her, roughly squeezing her jaw, the scent of something putrid on his breath. "You will never amount to anything, Elspeth Summerfield. Do you understand me? You will be a failure, and you will always be what you are now. A nothing."

Her papers fell from her hands as Grandfather stalked

away. Megan's mouth had dropped, and Ellie had run back out the front door. Neither of them ever told her parents.

And even now, knowing that what he had done was incredibly cruel and that everyone would say to let it go, that her grandfather was a bitter, hateful man, his words stayed within her. They were a wound healed over with bitter scars.

Where is my worth? What is my value?

Could it be bought by service? Did it come from her looks? Would it be found in some African hut as she cared for dying children?

Despite everyone's saying that a person's worth was not found in these things, Ellie couldn't let go of the belief that it was. And she now fulfilled her grandfather's prophecy. Now the disfigured within her had come to the surface. The inside was clearly visible for all to see.

Ellie's phone rang on the bed beside her head.

"Cramps?" Will asked sarcastically.

"Yeah. You can't understand."

"Oh, I understand. Get ready. I'm taking you out."

"Funny."

But his voice wasn't joking.

"It's a Friday night. I'll be there in two hours. Your mom already said yes."

"No, I'm not going." But Ellie already knew she would be. Why not? Why keep hiding the monster that she was? "Where are we going?"

Chapter 16

THE OUTSIDER

The No-Longer-Anonymous Blog about Life at West
   Redding High

April 13

Comments:

   Who is Megan Summerfield? I only know Ellie. Are they
related?

* * *

Ellie stared at the good side of her face. The skin was
smooth and unblemished. The fairness of her skin had
bugged her before. Megan tanned more easily and had once
called her the Sunscreen Queen.

   Turning her head to the mangled skin on her left side,
she stared for a long time. It wasn't a shock to look at it anymore. But how would other people see it on first view? It
reminded her of a candle that had melted and then grown
hard again. You could see some of the ridges and lines
where the skin was damaged and where they'd first tried
the dermabrasion technique. Her face was healing, and in a
few months they'd perform another surgery, tear everything up and wait for healing again. They'd do surgery after

surgery until her wounds looked the best the plastic surgeons could do.

A knock sounded on the bathroom door.

"Are you almost out?" Megan asked.

"We have more than one bathroom."

"All my stuff is in there."

Ellie pulled up her black sweats, pausing a moment to view the smooth skin on her right hip and thigh. The surgeons would soon take squares of this good skin to try covering the bad along her entire left side. It made her think of making papier-mâché masks in grade school: cutting up strips of newspaper, dipping them in the gloppy paste, and laying them on a balloon to form the mask. She'd have a mask made from her butt and thighs. The seams would go away eventually, the doctor told her. But that area wouldn't be smooth and unblemished as it was now. Instead of getting better, she'd always have to endure pain to improve. Nothing was patched up without some kind of pain.

She unlocked the door.

"What are you doing in there?" Megan asked, hands on her hips.

"Smoking crack."

"You know, I really don't like your sarcasm."

"What's that supposed to mean?"

"It was in English. *No comprende?*"

"You didn't like me before, you don't like me now—what's new?"

Megan shook her head.

Ellie turned to the mirror, suddenly self-conscious beneath the bright bathroom lights. She flipped off the main light and pulled her hair forward to cover her neck. It wouldn't fall enough to completely cover the side of her face, but it helped.

"When Will gets here, tell him I can't go," she said.

"Is that right?" He was standing behind Megan.

Ellie jumped when she saw him.

"Agoraphobic now?"

"No," she said.

"Yes," Megan said, motioning for Ellie to leave the bathroom. "But she doesn't know what that means. Remember, my sister was perfect and had everything going for her. Why would she fill her mind with vocabulary that included phobias?"

"A cruel sister. Do you find your approach motivating to her?" Will asked.

Megan paused. "I don't see it as cruelty. Perhaps unsympathetic honesty. I like who she is now better than before."

"Because of your issues or hers?"

Megan put her hands on her hips. "That would be both, Dr. Carl Jung."

Will smiled at that as Ellie glanced back and forth between the two of them. She didn't know what *agoraphobic* was. The fear of something. And who was Carl Jung—some famous psychotherapist or something?

"Agoraphobia is the fear of leaving your house," Megan said, again motioning for Ellie to leave the bathroom.

Ellie nodded, feeling a sudden weight of tiredness. They could label her whatever they wanted, but it wasn't accurate. She wasn't afraid of leaving her house. She was afraid of any and every single set of eyes landing on any part of her. What was that? Eyesaphobia? Sightaphobia? Perhaps she could find a cute blind guy to date. That wasn't a bad idea, actually.

"I have nothing to wear."

"Jeans, T-shirt."

"Jeans hurt me."

"Wear something of mine," Megan said.

"Make her come too," Ellie said to Will.

"I'll come," Megan said, guiding Ellie from the bathroom.

"Get ready, then, ladies. You need your public unveiling sometime."

Ellie thought again about what to wear. "Will it be dark?"

Will acted like he was looking out the window to inspect the night. "Looks dark, since it is night."

"No, at the place we're going to."

"Why?" he asked, as if daring her to admit that she didn't want people to see her.

"Forget it," she said. "I'm going to ask Megan what she's wearing."

"I bet you never thought you'd ask that question."

They both smiled at that.

＊ ＊ ＊

Ellie followed Will and Megan through a large dirt parking area, keeping her head tilted. The hat she wore helped to keep her hair falling forward to cover a good portion of her scars. People milled around their cars; a few others moved forward toward the low lighting coming from the trees.

"What is this place?"

"It's called Jonah's Farm. This guy from the Bay Area— some former dot-commer—moved up here and bought this farm, sort of an organic hippie deal. Every weekend he lets people come hang out, listen to music, whatever. They're going to have their first music festival in the summer."

Megan appeared familiar with this place as well. So this was where they went on the weekends? Jonah's Farm?

Ellie saw that this wasn't a gathering for jocks and cheer-leaders or drinkers of appletinis or those who enjoyed beer-drinking games. Smoke lingered in the air. A group of guys and girls walked together, wearing clothing that looked more seventies than the seventies.

Will carried a large, thick blanket, and Megan a thermos of something. Ellie shivered and stayed close to them. It was dark in the parking lot, but they were moving to an area with lanterns and more people.

They came to the top of a sloping hill with a large wooden stage at the bottom. People lounged around the base of the stage. Off to one side a guy was cooking on a giant grill. Someone played a harmonica. There had to be a hundred people or more.

"Over here," Will said, moving among people till he laid out the blanket in an empty spot.

He and Megan said hello to several people, nodded to some others. Ellie tried to act as if everything was normal, but she felt as if her face were a beacon for eyes and whis-pered discussions—though she didn't actually see anyone looking twice her way.

They had just settled onto the blanket when the guy at the giant barbecue grill jumped onto the stage and tapped the microphone.

"I guess that means it's on," he said with a laugh. He was

in his thirties, she guessed, and wore baggy jeans and a loose-fitting gray shirt.

"That's Jonah," Will said.

Jonah took the microphone in hand. "We're going to get started, so I'll be shutting down the grill until after our singer. We've still got kabobs with shrimp and mushrooms."

What is this? Ellie wondered. It reminded her of youth group gatherings or camp, where they'd sit outside and someone would play the guitar. It made her miss those days, the great sense of peace, with the stars bright overhead and God so near. She looked up. The stars were there, as if waiting for her to finally notice.

"Our featured artist tonight is Cara Lee."

A girl in her early twenties hopped up cheerily to the microphone. "Thanks for having me." She did a little dip. Her hair was in short pigtails with flared-out ends and red polka-dot ribbons. Her dress reminded Ellie of Dorothy from *The Wizard of Oz,* only toned down a bit.

"I love being in Redding again."

The crowd clapped loudly at that.

"You didn't tell me this would be, like, professional," Ellie said, leaning toward Will.

"It's not."

Cara Lee sang in a high, sweet voice as she strummed her guitar. She sounded folksy with a touch of rock, and strangely innocent and endearing. When the audience cheered, she smiled with shy pleasure.

"I brought some of my artwork this year. You can see it in Jonah's gallery in the converted barn. I stayed the past two winters in a little town in Wyoming and learned how to do some glassblowing. The vases are filled with various representations of the people and experiences I've had in the past four years of traveling. I call them my Life Vases, and I hope you'll check them out after the show."

The next song was about a dog and a hobo traveling a midnight train.

As Cara Lee sang, the sadness in the tone suddenly made Ellie want to cry. She thought of how so much happened on the fringe of what she'd been aware of. Her life had been constant activity, controlled chaos, scheduled events of homework, family, school events, church activities. Everything was about doing, instead of about being.

This world, the world Cara Lee sang about, was about being, expressing, breathing in life with all its good and bad. This was a world she hadn't seen. And didn't know she wanted to see.

As Cara Lee continued playing her guitar, she said, "I've been traveling around to bluegrass festivals and little gatherings like this all my life. People seem to like my music and my experiments in art. And only in the past year or so have I started telling a bit about my story. I guess our stories are as important as our songs and our art. Guess our stories are our art."

People clapped, and a few yelled and whistled.

"So I have a little story to tell about a girl who loved her father and spent years on the road with him, sitting on his guitar case while he made music. A few times they were pretty poor, and she quickly learned to sing with her daddy because that brought more dollars into the jar. And sometimes they were doing pretty well, and it looked like they might get a house and she could go to school and make friends, like the other girls she saw in towns all over this great country."

She strummed, then picked at the guitar's strings, picking up speed as the audience clapped in rhythm.

"He taught me how to play and how to listen to people from every walk of life. He was a lover of life. But when I was eleven, our time together came to an end—at least on this earth." She paused then, picking at the guitar in a gentle little tune. "Most people don't even notice . . ." Her voice trailed off, and she held up her hand. She was missing two fingers.

There was a reaction that rippled through the crowd.

"We were on a riverboat. He'd been booked as the entertainment, me as the usual backup. The boat driver was drunk and hit some old bridge pilings. I was trapped. My dad was a hero as usual." She kind of shrugged then, as if the audience could fill in the missing parts.

Ellie could vividly imagine Cara Lee as a girl with pigtails, her fingers crushed and her small body trapped as her father fought to save her and others before being swept down into the cold waters.

"I only tell that story because I know there are people here in all sorts of dark places for various reasons. And you know, we can do great things with whatever we've got going on."

The audience cheered, and a few people stood up, and then more. Ellie couldn't get her legs to move. She felt chills crawl over her skin. Anger burned in her throat. How could Will bring her here to listen to this? If he looked at her with any kind of smug expression, she'd slap him. But Will was standing with his face toward the stage. And from the corner of her eye, Ellie saw her sister still on the edge of the blanket, turning away and wiping her eyes.

As Cara Lee returned to the music and the audience relaxed back against their blankets, Will reached a hand to cover Ellie's. He didn't look at her or say a word, simply rested his hand over hers and after a while wove his fingers through hers. The simple touch sent waves of emotion— everything from embarrassment, wondering what others would think of this good-looking guy with the deformed girl, to warmth and a longing to rest her head against his chest, and also to anger at a world so filled with pain and sorrow. She held it all in, clenching her jaw even though it hurt, afraid to let even a single tear go for fear she'd be undone and never stop crying.

After the concert they walked to what was once a barn but now could pass for any gallery in a metropolitan city. Ellie stayed between Megan and Will.

"Why didn't he come?" Will asked Megan.

She held up her phone a bit. "Couldn't get off work in time."

Ellie glanced at her sister but didn't ask. Megan and Will knew a number of people, who greeted Ellie with complete indifference when they were introduced. She had a few moments of forgetting about her face. Then she'd remember and shy away.

Cara Lee's vases were beautiful, funky, cute, twisted. One was filled with colored cuts of glass and had a light shining from behind. It was called *Jenny*. The black vase had rocks and razors attached to the glass. It was called *Last Night in LA*.

Though Ellie wanted to talk to Cara Lee, she stayed away from the cluster of people surrounding the artist. The old Ellie would have waited and eventually gone up to her, told her how much she enjoyed her music. But that old Ellie wouldn't know true inspiration because she'd yet to know true pain. Now, she knew, Cara Lee would look her in the face and understand. No words would need to be exchanged, no small talk or surface questions about her art or the next place she'd be singing.

And that was exactly why Ellie stayed away.

Megan was talking to some people she didn't know, and Ellie's body was throbbing from the left to the right. She needed to go soon. This was the longest she'd been out.

"So what did you think?" Will asked.

"I guess you had a purpose for bringing me tonight? Make me see that a disability shouldn't stop me?"

"Did it work?"

She wanted to shoot something back, but the truth was, it *had* inspired her. She shrugged her shoulders.

"I didn't know she'd say all of that. Just wanted you to come with me. I told you, I'm taking advantage of this friendship."

"Cigarette," she muttered, unable to tease him back. The pain must have shone in her eyes. "I need to go home now."

"I'll get Megan."

"What are you doing?" Megan grabbed the cigarette out of Ellie's hand as soon as she saw it.

"It helps," Ellie said. The pain was raging, and she wondered if she could walk all the way to the car.

"What are you, stupid?" Megan was cursing at Will as he

helped Ellie walk. Finally he picked her up, which made her cry out, and carried her the rest of the way to the car.

"Guess I know how to end the night," Ellie whispered with her eyes closed as he set her into the front passenger seat.

It was 3:00 a.m. She'd never gone home that late before. Both she and Megan would have been grounded if their parents had woken up and caught them. Ellie was a little disappointed that they didn't.

Chapter 17

THE OUTSIDER
The No-Longer-Anonymous Blog about Life at West
   Redding High
April 21

"The most difficult way is, in the long run, the easiest."
—*The Books in My Life*, Henry Miller

So I shouldn't buy those DVDs on "Making Millions without
Doing a Thing" in twenty easy payments of $19.99?

* * *

The next week moved along like the one before: physical
therapy, television and more movies, reading about
celebrities on the Internet, hanging out with Megan and
Will, browsing through her friends' MySpace and Facebook
pages. There was a note on her MySpace—though she hadn't
updated it since before the accident.

Ryan's friend Bly had written her: *We miss you, Ellie.
You're remembered every day. Come back sometime.*

She thought about writing him, but it might open a door
she wasn't prepared for, so she read about who was dating
whom, about the latest parties, the nostalgic notes about

how soon they'd be graduating and how life would change forever. Ryan's MySpace page was down, which she found strange. Tara's had pictures of her and Ryan at the prom. He was incredibly good-looking in his tux, and Ellie felt a pang of jealousy.

She gave a halfhearted effort to her homework. The home teacher, Mr. Carr, didn't seem to notice. He praised her work and encouraged her to finish up her past assignments so she'd be on track to graduate in June. It seemed too easy, in a way. But then, she wasn't trying for college scholarships now, though Mr. Carr and her mother continued to drop hints and encouragements about different schools she could apply to.

When she'd talked with Maggie in her counseling session that week, Ellie spent the hour talking about her first outing instead of the stages of grief and her grandfather. Maggie thought it was progress.

On Friday, Will picked Ellie and Megan up again. Her old clothes were baggy on her, since she'd lost so much weight in the hospital. She took a pain pill before she left this time. Ellie was surprised when she walked outside to rain. She'd been living in a confined area too long.

"Are we still going to Jonah's Farm?" Ellie asked when they got in the car.

"It's canceled."

They went instead to a party at a small, funky house near downtown. Ellie didn't want to go in. She'd been out more and more with her appointments and last weekend at Jonah's Farm. But this was confined, people jammed into a house.

"Come on," Will said, pulling her arm. "It's better in the back."

Ellie kept her head down. She hoped she wouldn't see anyone she knew, but the people looked college age and older.

"Where'd Megan go?" she asked when they reached the back patio. It was empty except for a few people at the opposite end, smoking cigarettes. The house was on a hill and gave a view of the city lights and buildings.

"She's with James."

"Who?"

Will shook his head. "You still don't know your sister?"

"I guess not." Ellie looked around, wondering what they were doing here. Though Will and Megan were the two people Ellie was around the most now, there was still an enormous amount she didn't know about them. Like how did they know these people or hear about these parties? And as close as she and Megan had become, neither of them talked about the guys in their lives.

"Are you okay? Sorry this is so crowded." Will tapped out a cigarette and lit it.

Ellie took it from him.

"Great. I'll get chewed out by your sister again."

She ignored him and took a drag. It was something to do, and it made her feel better. "Sometimes I wish I could go to the Island of Misfit Toys."

He raised his eyebrow in question, then took her cigarette and inhaled it. "We'll share this one. After it, we'll both quit, okay?"

"Yeah, yeah."

"Now back to your misfit island—" He handed her the cigarette.

"You know, on *Rudolph the Red-Nosed Reindeer*. There's the island for all the toys that are broken or made wrong that Santa can't give to the good little girls and boys. The misfits. So they stick them all on that island."

"Like a leper colony."

She frowned. "I was thinking it sounded like a safe place."

"Maybe the lepers thought so too," Will said, and Ellie thought for a moment he might kiss her then, the way he leaned close.

She stepped back suddenly and glanced around. No way did she want any attention drawn their way.

"Speaking of misfits," Will said, "did you see who's sitting by the stereo?"

"Who?"

"Take a look."

Through the sliding glass window, Ellie saw him—leaning against the wall by himself. Ryan. His eyes were closed as he listened to the music, and his head moved slightly to the beat.

Her heart skipped and she backed away, afraid he might see her. But he was lost in his own little world. If she'd been in the living room, standing in front of him, Ellie doubted that Ryan would notice her.

"Is he stoned?" she asked.

"Fried would be more accurate, I think."

Ellie hadn't seen Ryan since the hospital. She wondered if Tara was there too. This was supposed to be a place she didn't have to worry about seeing people she knew.

"Why is he here?"

Will shrugged and turned back to the railing. Ellie stepped closer to the window. Some people walked by, but no one paid attention to Ryan sitting alone on the floor. He looked sad, and Ellie put her hand against the glass as she watched him. Should she go help him? she wondered. There came a quick flash of memory to the last party they'd both been to. The last one before . . .

"You can talk to him if you want," Will said in that sort of permission-granting way that couples have with one another. He was leaning on the railing, looking out over the city with a new cigarette in his hand. So much for quitting.

What would she say to Ryan? She was worried about him here. Who did he know? How would he get home?

Ellie wanted to ask Will why he'd brought her here, but she knew it was partly her fault. She didn't want to go to a movie, or a restaurant or a play. Not with the chance being high of seeing someone. And she just wasn't ready for the attention, for the first stares and her old friends acting as if she looked just the same.

"You know, I don't even like parties. I didn't go to them before," she said, glancing again at Ryan.

"We could go somewhere else."

Ellie sent Megan a text:

Mind leaving?
Megan: I'll get a ride.
Ellie: Who with?
Megan: Talk about it tomorrow. I'm fine, go ahead.
     Don't wait up.

Ellie: Ryan's here.

Megan: Yeah. James knows him. He'll give him a
    ride home.

"Who exactly is James?" Ellie asked Will.

"He's your sister's boyfriend, sort of."

"O-kay." Ellie shook her head. "Ready?"

When they walked through the living room, Ellie paused momentarily in front of Ryan. She wanted to ask him what he was doing there and how he had been since they last talked. She wanted to help him. He looked up then, and Ellie quickly followed after Will.

"Will he be okay?" Ellie asked when they reached the car.

Will paused, then clicked the doors unlocked. "You want to give him a ride home?"

She thought *yes* but said no.

"What do you want to do now?"

Ellie shrugged as they got into the car. "Guess I'm not the most fun to be around once we leave my house."

Will looked at his phone to see the time. "It's not even eleven. We could get movies and ice cream or play *Terminal Warfare* or whatever you want."

"Movies, ice cream, and video games. I actually played a lot of video games in the hospital."

Will drove down the hilly street, and though she was still worried about Ryan and wondered why he was there without Tara in sight, her mood lightened the farther away they went.

Will spoke. "I'd say we could go to my house, but I think my dad is home."

"Are you ever going to tell me about Brazil?"

"I don't know why you're so curious about it."

"Since fourth grade, I've wondered what happened."

He laughed. "Do you want a Dutch Bros. or Starbucks before we go back to your house?"

"Just ice cream."

"And I suppose you want me to go into the store alone and buy it?"

She gave him a smile. "Sorry."

"Then I get to pick what kind. My favorite is fruitcake."

"There's no fruitcake ice cream."

They made up flavors until he parked at the store.

Sitting in the car waiting, Ellie thought about Ryan. The sadness in his face haunted her. What was happening with him? She thought about texting him, but he probably wouldn't see it tonight anyway, in the condition he was in. He'd always been antidrugs, though he drank a lot before they started dating.

When Will got back, he asked, "Have you been crying?"

She shook her head. "So what kind did you get?"

"Onion."

Will dropped her off while he went to his house for movies and the game console. She found Dad hunched over his desk with his forehead resting on his hand. Stacks of opened bills were piled around his elbow.

"You're home early," he said as he rubbed his eyes.

"Are those my hospital bills?"

He nodded.

"Are we going to be okay?"

"Yes, honey. Don't worry." He turned in his chair. "You

know, we all expect everything to be good in our lives. But what about all the days that bad things could have happened, but didn't? We don't realize all the potential for bad in our lives."

She frowned. "That's comforting."

He chuckled and rubbed his eyes again. "Guess that didn't come out as encouraging as I hoped. I just mean that we should be thankful for what God does in our lives. The good and the bad shouldn't change how we feel about Him. We don't even know all the times He's saved us from things."

Ellie didn't care to hear about God right now, but she was suddenly struck by one fact. "You aren't anything like Grandfather."

"I've tried to be as different from my father as I could possibly be. Sometimes I've gone too far the other way. I know I can be too passive."

"I think you're perfect." Ellie smiled at him.

He winked back. "And you have a lot of people who love you, Ellie."

She nodded. "I know."

"Do you know that your sister slept in your bedroom every night while you were in the hospital?"

"She did?"

"And one of Ryan's little sisters rode her bike over three or four times to ask how you were doing."

"When?"

"While you were in Sacramento." Dad's chair creaked as he leaned back. "People really look up to you."

"They did look up to me."

"No. You don't see it, honey. But they still look up to you and always will."

Ellie sighed, wondering what to say to that. Will's knock on the door saved her from hearing more. "We're going to watch a movie."

"Okay, honey."

* * *

"Why do you want to be with me?" Megan asked James. She took a drag of her cigarette and wished she'd never started up the habit again. Why had she started up the habit of James again too? After everything, she should be making better choices with her life. But when it came time to choose something in the moment, Megan always ended up doing what she didn't really want.

James laughed, which always cut through her serious mood.

"I'm serious," she said but couldn't stop the slight grin.

He pulled her toward him. "What do you want, babe? What do you want from me?"

She shrugged and leaned on the railing of the balcony outside his apartment. All she knew was that this wasn't the life she wanted. She didn't know what life she did want, but this wasn't it. They didn't go to the movies or out for a nice dinner; they didn't go into the city or walk the Sundial Bridge or do "normal people" things—though she didn't want to be normal. She didn't know what she wanted to be.

"Is this about the opening?" he asked with a smug grin.

"No," she said.

They'd gone to a gallery opening, and the artist was a

former girlfriend of James. She'd kissed him full-on in front of Megan, and everyone acted as if this was normal, and if she acted upset, then it was her problem. No one was shocked by anything. No one judged. Well, at least, they didn't judge each other. They could sleep around, drink, do drugs, get pierced and tattooed, whatever.

"I think Lyla liked you as much as she liked me."

Megan knew what he meant by that. Lyla had held her a few seconds too long when they left. "I bet you liked that."

He laughed. "Why not?"

"And how many girlfriends have you had in your twenty years?"

"More than a few. Why, jealous?"

"You'd like that too," she said, which made him laugh harder. She sighed. "You didn't answer me."

"What was the question? Why do I want to be with you?"

She dropped her cigarette butt into the coffee can and watched the smoke drift up. James was taking way too long answering this.

"You're hot. And I mean, really hot."

"There're a lot of hot girls in the world."

"This is true." He nodded and grinned. "I want to be with you because you make me want to write songs, play my guitar, create . . ."

She didn't want to hear more. "Do you have another cigarette?"

Megan remained on the balcony for now, but inwardly she was walking away. The problem was, she had no idea what she was walking toward.

* * *

The next afternoon, Ellie's phone rang the default ring. She still hadn't set up any ringtones. Staring at the number, she nearly let it go to voice mail. Then she picked it up and said hello.

Ryan's voice was low and so quiet she had to hold the phone close to her ear to hear him.

"I thought I saw you last night, though it's taken all day to believe it wasn't my imagination."

"Maybe it was your imagination," she said softly.

"It was you."

"You weren't looking so good."

He sighed, and Ellie realized how much she'd missed his voice. "And I'm paying for it today. I want to talk to you."

Ellie pulled the little purple dog from beneath her pillow. She'd thought of washing it to remove the scent of smoke and fuel, but she wanted that smell to remain for now. "Go ahead and talk, then."

"I want to talk to you in person."

Ellie groaned. Why couldn't people just give her the space to grow stronger again? Perhaps someday she'd be closer to the Ellie everyone knew and loved. But she was far from there.

"Ryan . . ." She didn't know how to finish or what to say.

"It'll take five minutes, that's all."

"I have someone coming over right now."

"Who? Will Stefanos?" he asked with hurt evident in his tone.

"Yeah."

205

"I can't come over, but weird Will can?"

"I fit with the weird kids now." She said it as lightly as possible, though the truth wasn't lost on either of them. Ellie could picture Ryan with his head resting in his hands, and then he'd push back his hair in frustration. She did miss him, all the things about him. But what was the point of continuing something that would only hurt someone, probably both of them?

"You were breaking up with me the night of the accident."

"We had a fight."

"No. And this is something I've figured out about you, Ellie."

"What is that?"

"You can be there for everyone. You can be the best friend, the confidant, the one people seek in an emergency. You keep secrets, and you'd give your last dime if someone was in need. But when you think *you* might need someone or you're getting too close, then you pull away. You're nice about it, but you run."

"Interesting theory. Thanks for telling me."

"You're proving my point."

"Maybe I just didn't see a future for us."

"I don't doubt that. You never opened yourself to the possibility."

"I'm sorry if all this has been so hard for you," she said sarcastically.

"You sound like Megan."

"Funny."

"I'm not joking."

It was unsettling to hear Ryan sound jaded.

"You can't hide away forever, running from everyone and everything."

You wanna bet? Ellie thought. "What am I supposed to do?"

"Get on MySpace, text your friends, come back to school."

"Okay," she said. But there was no way she would do all that. She'd checked her MySpace a few times. She'd seen the Web site about her. The old pictures of her and all her friends' notes brought tears to her eyes. It was still too soon.

If only she could disappear for a while. Maybe she could go stay with some far-off relative and not deal with the old world making her feel guilty. They wanted Ellie back, but she wasn't that Ellie now. And she'd never be. And was it right for her to just return as if nothing had happened, as if the scars covering her body weren't there? Stasia couldn't come back. Was she so quickly forgotten?

Neither she nor Ryan spoke for so long that Ellie wondered if he'd fallen asleep.

"When you want to talk, I'm here," he said.

"Thanks. But I doubt your girlfriend wants you talking to me very much."

"My girlfriend?"

"You're going to tell me you aren't going out with Tara?"

He sighed, sounding annoyed. "At least she wants me. Call if you need me. Bye, Els."

She set down the phone and hugged the little dog to her chest. She'd still never talked to Ryan about Purple. It seemed another thing better left unsaid.

* * *

Ellie and Will watched episode after episode of the first season of *Heroes* in her room. Ellie had never seen it before, with all of her nighttime school and church activities. Now she was quickly drawn in and hooked on the characters, who all displayed abilities that sometimes were more like *dis*abilities.

"My friends are getting mad at me," Ellie said during a break as she carried an overflowing bowl of popcorn from the kitchen back upstairs.

"Nice friends." He carried the drinks.

"They think I'm ignoring them."

"Which you are."

"Yes, which I am."

"And they should understand. Or try to."

Will set the drinks down on the nightstand, then reached for a handful of popcorn and went back to close the door. Not only did her parents allow Will free access to her bedroom for huge segments of time without anyone checking on them, but he lay on the bed like it was his own recliner.

They hadn't talked about the kiss or kissed again. Sometimes Ellie wondered why he didn't try. Whenever she thought of initiating anything, she thought of how she looked and felt ridiculous. Maybe Will really only saw her as a friend.

"Ryan called me today," she said quickly as she took her spot on the bed, lying on her stomach with her head at the bottom.

Will tossed a popcorn kernel into the air and caught it with his mouth. "Glad he made it home alive last night."

Ellie didn't like how he'd said that, considering everything. "If you were really worried about him—"

"I wasn't worried about him."

Sometimes she wanted to see a streak of jealousy in Will. Some show of protectiveness, instead of writing off Ryan as if he was no competition whatsoever.

But then, why would he be jealous over his maimed friend, or whatever it was they were to each other?

Ellie saw him looking at his phone a number of times as if expecting a call. "Got someplace to go?"

"Not yet," he said.

She sat up. "You're going out?"

"Yeah, I think. A friend is home from college for the weekend. She's going to UC-Santa Cruz, where I'm going next year."

"She?" Ellie couldn't believe this. She'd assumed he would stay late like he usually did and then go home, not out.

"You don't mind, do you?"

It wasn't like they were dating. They had no commitment, so what could she say? "I don't care what you do."

"Great. I was thinking of meeting her at that new coffeehouse downtown."

"That'll be fun," Ellie stated dryly.

"I can see if it's a place you'd want to go, or if it's too crowded."

That was it. She didn't want him there any longer.

"You want to watch another episode?"

"No. Why don't you go meet your friend?"

"Okay." He took another handful of popcorn and left. She heard him say good-bye to her parents, who were watching TV downstairs.

Ellie jumped up and paced her room. Spotting the little paper birds sitting on her desk, she took her fist and smashed one, then another, until they all lay flat and crumpled.

"I hate his stupid birds. I hate him!" And she cursed under her breath and smashed another already flattened bird.

After a few minutes, she picked one up. Its wings were sprawled out, its beak twisted. It reminded her of the book about the seagull who wanted to fly better and higher than all the others.

She grabbed the box from the accident off her desk and hurled it across the room.

And the rage inside continued. She thought of Stasia reaching for the stereo just as that deer stepped out. And then she died. Just like that, her life was over. Was that better or worse than the suffering Ellie now lived with?

Ellie's parents were so stupid for always trusting her, always thinking she'd make the right choices, always expecting the best. And what was up with Ryan suddenly analyzing her—she hated that, hated *him* for trying to figure her out. What business did he have saying things like that to her? And where was Megan tonight—out with some boyfriend she'd never told her sister about? They were supposed to be close now. Then she thought of her old friends and the school faculty and administration, that stupid girl who still e-mailed, wanting to put on a rally in Ellie's honor . . .

Ellie wanted to scream, to make her hate list, to get it all said or shouted or to hurt someone. Maybe she'd text Will and tell him to never come back. She fell back onto her bed and closed her eyes. The rage inside settled down, and weariness took over. She got up and went to take a bath.

Beautiful

Awhile later, as she watched TV, her phone beeped.

Will: Still sulking?
Ellie: No.
Will: What r u doing?
Ellie: Watching Heroes.
Will: Without me?
Ellie: You left.
Will: Ah, don't be that way.
Ellie: I'm not.
Will: She's a friend.
Ellie: How old?
Will: Twenty-two. And yes, attractive. But I'm not
      attracted. She's like a big sister.

Ellie clenched her jaw and threw the phone down. It beeped a moment later.

Will: Don't be jealous.
Ellie: I'm not!
Will: Yes, you are.

And she wondered if she was.

Will: I would have stayed if you had asked.
Ellie: I only wanted you to stay if you wanted to.
Will: I wanted to stay, but I wanted you to want me
      there.
Ellie: Okay.
Will: I miss you.

She smiled.

Chapter 18

THE OUTSIDER

The No-Longer-Anonymous Blog about Life at West
   Redding High

May 3

I've been busy. Finals are coming. So I'm writing quotes, that's
something, and very helpful. So here's today's:

"Carpe Diem" (Seize the Day). —Horace

Let's do!

* * *

Ellie sat in her pajamas and ate syrup-drenched waffles
and crisp bacon with her parents on Sunday morning
while Mom called again and again for Megan to hurry up for
church. Ellie promised she'd watch the service online as usual.

"I still don't like it. Honey, make your daughter come to
church with us."

"One more month, 'k? Then I'll probably go," Ellie said
and somewhat meant it.

"She'll come when she's ready, dear," Dad said as he
poured Mom and Ellie more coffee.

Mom frowned. "Everyone asks about you."

"Well, tell every single one that I appreciate it and wish I could be there."

Megan was coming down the stairs and acted like she was gagging over Ellie's words.

"You better hurry up, Megan, or you won't get any waffles before church," Ellie said with a grin.

Twenty minutes later, Ellie stood at the door with a cup of coffee in her hand and smiled triumphantly at Megan as she walked past to join their parents in the car.

"You're good. It's pretty conniving to use your accident to stay away from church."

Ellie shrugged. "What can I say? If you've got it, use it."

"But unlike me, you actually like church."

Ellie didn't respond but turned back inside. Megan was wrong. She *liked* church, past tense. Now she didn't know if she liked or disliked it. She hadn't been there in months, and though at times she felt a sense of God being with her, mostly He was either so far away or He'd never existed in the first place.

Listening to the sermon, Ellie wanted to tell her pastor that she had made the right decisions. She didn't drink or do drugs. She was still a virgin. She'd gone on a mission trip, been a winter camp counselor, been "involved." And that didn't count any of her school activities. She had given her entire life to doing good things. So why hadn't God saved her from all of this? Where was God when she was trapped inside that car?

The pastor talked about faith, and she picked up enough to pass the Q&A Mom would give her when she got home. The churchy language bugged her. All the things people said to their family and to Ellie in cards and e-mails:

God's not finished with you yet.

God has a plan for your life.

He saved you for a purpose.

We thank God for saving you.

There is always something to be grateful for, even in our darkest hours.

When God closes a door, He opens a window. That one didn't make any sense to her at all.

The pastor said, "We say that we believe in God. But only when your faith is tested do you really find the measure of your faith."

Ellie closed her laptop and turned on the TV. She wasn't going to let the God stuff get her down. Today, she felt pretty good . . . actually, *really* good. Stronger, healthier, and without pain.

The house was quiet and all her own for an hour or two. She padded barefoot to the office, looking for a piece of paper. She wanted to make a plan for redecorating her room, and there were supplies she needed for a sewing project Megan was going to help her with.

On Dad's desk calendar, her name caught her eye. Thursday. 9:00 a.m. Surgery.

The waffles suddenly knotted in her stomach, and her mouth tasted sickly sweet.

Four days. Another surgery in four days. Mom had reminded her recently that another surgery was coming. And Ellie had done everything to ignore it. Life was finding a rhythm, and she wasn't ready to interrupt it.

This surgery would be on her face again.

She'd be starting over. They'd peel off the papier-mâché

scars that weren't as bright and raw as before, and her healing would start over again. The ointment, the missing skin, the itching, the bright red evidence of her injury. The pain.

Someone was knocking on the front door.

Ellie walked toward the door with heavy steps. She was turning the knob when she remembered that she never answered the door—not since the accident. She wanted to slam it shut and peek through the side window to see who it was, but it was too late.

Opening the door a crack, she peered out.

"Hello, Ellie." It was Stasia's mom, and as soon as she saw Ellie's face, Mrs. Fuller started crying.

Ellie opened the door and let her in.

"I'm so sorry. I didn't think I would cry."

Mrs. Fuller wiped her eyes with the Kleenex Ellie gave to her. She sat on the couch, and Ellie put on the teakettle, hoping for a distraction. Perhaps this would be a simple little visit, and Ellie could get back to finding ways to delay the upcoming surgery.

"It's okay. It's understandable." She hoped the kettle would whistle soon.

"I've wanted to see you for a while." Mrs. Fuller wiped her eyes again. "But I just couldn't. Did you get my flowers in the hospital?"

"I think so." Ellie really didn't remember. So many people had sent balloons and flowers that it was hard to keep track. Mom had sent the thank-you cards.

"Oh, that's fine. I just didn't want you to think anything bad because you hadn't heard from our family."

Ellie knew what she meant. Mrs. Fuller didn't want Ellie

or her family wondering if Stasia's family harbored any resentment toward them because Ellie had lived and Stasia had died.

Mrs. Fuller folded her hands. Her eyes were just like Stasia's. "You were the last person to see her alive. Just being here with you is really nice for me."

Ellie shifted uncomfortably on the chair, glancing at the clock. Her family wouldn't be back for another hour or more if they went to lunch or if Mom talked after church.

"Ellie. Do you remember what happened?"

This was the question she'd hoped to avoid. She wished people would think the accident had been wiped from her memory. That happened all the time to accident victims. If only it had happened to her. Instead, Ellie remembered nearly every detail, even if a sort of thick, surreal fog surrounded it all.

The teakettle whistled in the kitchen.

Ellie nodded, and Mrs. Fuller moved forward to the edge of the couch, waiting.

What should I say? Ellie wondered. The images came back. She and Stasia were side by side, one dead and one alive. What made one of them chosen and one of them not?

Stasia had loved horses and animals. She had to test her insulin level, eat healthy, worry about the future her disease might cause. Now she was dead. Surely her mother had worried about her daughter as mothers do. And none of that mattered now. The worst had happened.

"It happened really fast," Ellie said.

"Was it a deer?"

Ellie nodded. She remembered how it felt like hours before anyone came at all, but she knew it was only minutes. The wait for the paramedics was longer; she had no idea how long.

"Don't move her!"

"The car is on fire!"

"Will it blow up?"

"This door is jammed."

They couldn't get Stasia out. Someone had opened Ellie's door, helped to pull her away from the flames.

People were yelling, leaning over her, putting something over her arm and face. Finally the helicopter, a sound that came from beyond the voices and grew louder, like the answer to a cry for help. Who were those people who had helped?

"I just need to know," Mrs. Fuller said, with her hands shaking so badly she clenched them together.

Ellie understood. "She didn't suffer. I promise you. I think she was already gone before the . . . I think she passed away in the accident."

Mrs. Fuller covered her mouth with her hands and burst into tears. "Thank God. Oh, thank God," she said over and over as the kettle's whistle continued its lonesome cry.

Ellie answered Mrs. Fuller's questions and made them tea. The longer they talked, the less burdened the woman appeared. She asked Ellie about her studies and reminded her of the coming graduation.

Mrs. Fuller hugged Ellie gently. "I can't tell you what this has meant for me."

"It's been nice for me as well." And she meant it. Talking

about the accident with Stasia's mother was the closest she could come to talking to Stasia herself.

Before Mrs. Fuller left, she said to Ellie, "Don't let this be the end of your life. You have a lot of living to do."

Chapter 19

THE OUTSIDER

The No-Longer-Anonymous Blog about Life at West
   Redding High

May 17

Does every human have a purpose? I call people stupid, but
I include myself as well. But much of that is because we are
stupid. We have great potential and possibilities. We could
rise up and do great things. I often become trapped in the
immediate. I make choices based on what feels good now,
not what's good for me in the overall scheme of my life. Do
I have a purpose that I'm missing?

   I'm starting to believe in it. But one thing I also know,
humanity is flawed. And so, strangely, that brings me around
to the larger topic. God. It seems that only with God can
mankind discover and serve its purpose, collectively and
individually.

   Who would guess "The Outsider" would have a post
about God? But perhaps as graduation approaches, the bigger picture needs to be addressed.

* * *

The scissors came closer and closer to her head, and Ellie had a quick moment of panic. *Wait!* But she remained in the chair in her parents' master bathroom with the towel around her shoulders.

"It's time," she said with a fearful intake of air.

Consuela had been cutting Ellie's hair since she was ten and Ellie was preparing for a performance of *Swing Kids* at the small local theater.

"Oh, girl, we're going to shape up that hair in a nice style. You'll feel more like your old self again."

"I doubt that," Ellie said. It had been two weeks since her latest surgery. The pain was ebbing slowly again, and though the plastic surgeon said it went very well and would be the last one on her face for a while, she was starting the long healing process over again.

"I want something different," Ellie said.

Mom and Consuela glanced at one another.

Hiding her scars and trying to get back her old self was impossible. There was no recapturing who she'd been. Her parents expected it. She'd overheard Mom on the phone to someone—probably P Frank—saying that she'd thought Ellie would bounce back quicker. Ellie had never let anything get her down for long in the past. Her school counselor had stopped by as well. Everyone was expecting her to go back to school, take on all her old roles. But she was changed, and she didn't know what that meant for the new Ellie.

"Do you have something specific in mind?"

Ellie pointed to a magazine on the counter, open to a picture of Natalie Portman with her hair cut short. The sides were longer and fell toward her face. "People think I look like her, though of course now only half of my face looks like her."

Ellie laughed, but Consuela and Mom only looked horrified.

"Actually, three-fourths of your face looks like her," Megan said, flipping through a tabloid as she sat on the edge of the sunken tub.

"Megan," Mom scolded, but both girls grinned.

"Well, let's shape up that hair, then," Consuela said with a nervous chuckle.

Ellie watched as the long inches of hair fell to the floor. Panic swept over her, and images flashed before her eyes. Images of Stasia's face, of knives and axes, of arms and legs cut from bodies and dropping to the floor.

"Are you okay, honey?" Consuela asked, taking a step back and examining her face. "You're sweating."

The images faded, and Ellie wiped her forehead, feeling a line of sweat running down her chest. "Fine. I'm fine. Guess losing my hair is scarier than I thought."

Megan was frowning at her. Consuela went quickly back to cutting, and Ellie focused on her breathing and counted to a hundred, then a hundred backwards. Maggie would be proud, Ellie thought. She'd told Ellie to expect such things as post-trauma. It was all part of the lovely journey toward healing. Ellie would have to ask why "horrific images" wasn't one of the stages of grief.

* * *

Even Megan agreed that Ellie's haircut was a dramatic change. If she didn't know it was her own face in the mirror, Ellie might even think she looked attractive with her intriguing scars. Her dark hair curved toward her face, somewhat covering the scabbed-over flesh along her jawline. The scars along her neck were slightly more visible now, but everyone admired the change and commented on how professional and mature she looked.

"It's amazing how good it looks," Megan said later.

Ellie had come to her sister's room, bored in her own. Will was busy working with his father, doing landscape work. Megan was sitting on her bed, tearing up pieces of paper.

Ellie sat at the other end. "Consuela is pretty talented," she said. Today she was finding it a little painful to speak; the wound was cracking, and she needed to get more antibiotic cream.

Megan continued to rip the paper into smaller and smaller pieces.

"What is this?" Ellie asked, picking up a few pieces. Some were torn photographs.

"This is my relationship with James."

Ellie looked at the papers on the bed by Megan's leg. Letters and e-mails.

On the bedside table was a bowl with a thick liquid and a paintbrush.

"What are you doing?"

"Decoupage."

"You're making a decoupage out of your relationship with James?"

"My relationship with James is over. So I'm tearing it apart and making something new out of it. I'm decorating some jars." She picked up a glass votive.

The concept was pretty cool, Ellie had to admit. The

transforming of one thing into something else. Not forgotten, but changed.

"You are so ceremonious. People wouldn't guess that about you."

"People don't guess about me at all."

"So, did you love him?"

Megan shrugged. "I thought so. But I don't know."

Ellie nodded, then dropped her head, wanting to ask more but unsure where to begin.

"I've always felt guilty because of what Grandfather did to you."

Ellie's head jerked up, but Megan continued to tear paper as if she hadn't said a word. Before she could ask her to repeat it, Megan continued.

"Looking back, I guess we call it verbal abuse or mental abuse."

They had never once talked about this. Ellie had only told her parents bits and pieces, through tears and fear of what Grandfather would do or say if they confronted him. In her counseling sessions Ellie only danced around the subject, letting only slight memories be revealed.

She leaned her back against the wall and drew her legs up and wrapped her arms around her knees—then asked the question she had held inside all these years.

"Why did he hate me?" she whispered.

Megan paused a moment in her tearing. "Because you were like he used to be. And you looked like Grandma."

"I don't want to be like him. Why do people say that?"

"You were the good he used to be. Before the war and before he started drinking. Before Grandma left him."

Ellie shook her head. She couldn't see Grandfather as someone good.

Megan continued. "He was a really unhappy and angry person. After Grandma left him, he never got over it. He hated her with a passion. And then she died, and that only made it worse."

"How do you know all this?"

"Dad and Aunt Betty, and some I've figured out since I've gotten older. I was his favorite, but whether that was an honor or a curse, I don't know. He didn't exactly love me. I don't think he could love. And he saw Grandma when he looked at you. And in the things that you did, he saw who he'd once been, but wasn't anymore."

It didn't really make sense. How could an adult be so cruel to a child? How could hatred grow so deep and bitter that he'd hurt a child's heart without remorse? And yet Ellie could see the growth of bitterness within herself, and in Megan. They were the grandchildren of Edward Summerfield, after all.

"I hated you for a long time, you know."

Ellie nodded.

"You excelled at pretty much everything, which made me hate you all the more. I wanted to believe what he said about you."

Ellie didn't know what to say. To guess it was one thing, but to hear it spoken was like a quick turn of the knife.

"I'm sorry I didn't stick up for you."

"You were a kid too. And Grandfather was terrifying."

"But I loved it that he didn't like you. He was the only person who liked me better. Everyone, and I mean everyone, always liked you best. It sounds so ridiculously juvenile now. But at the time, I knew that only one person was on my side, and that was this hateful man who I could never really love."

Ellie stared down at the bits of paper. "Maybe I should make some decoupage stuff too."

Megan motioned to the bowl. "I have a lot of paste."

"You know, sister, your art is really fantastic. I never really noticed it until I had to share your room that week of Grandfather's funeral. Even then, I sort of brushed it off as weird, or too dark. But you're really good."

Megan smiled. "Thanks."

"Something is wrong with us."

"That we can't love?"

Ellie nodded. "Yeah."

"We can. We just need to stop being afraid."

* * *

"Graduation is a month away," Mom said, clicking away with her knitting needles as they watched a talent search TV show.

Megan wished it were a day away. She was ready to get on with her life, though she wasn't exactly sure what that meant. Ellie took a handful of chips from beside her and leaned her head on Megan's shoulder just the way she did when they were little. Megan pushed her shoulder up and nudged Ellie away, making Ellie laugh.

"Mr. Hanson called me today," Mom said in her most annoying singsong voice.

Ellie looked at Mom with naive interest. "Why? Is Megan valedictorian?"

Megan coughed and spit Diet Coke across the coffee table. She jumped up, laughing and coughing, and ran to the kitchen.

She overheard Mom say, "Why do you say things like that? You sound like her now." That made Megan smile.

She came back with a paper towel. Ellie kept her eyes on the television.

"Your classmates look up to you," Mom said. "I think the teachers do too. And they've done a lot for our family."

Ellie dropped her feet from the coffee table, muttering beneath her breath. She rose from the couch slowly, painfully.

"You aren't going off to your room, young lady."

"Mom, why do you care more about other people than about us? You always force us to do things to make everyone else feel good. What about me? What about *our* family?"

Megan looked from Ellie to Mom. *Go, El.*

Mom's face reflected shock. She stared at Ellie and stuttered to explain. "I always care about our family first."

"It never seems like it to me."

Ellie glanced at Megan for support, but Megan didn't want to contribute. Mom wouldn't listen if she said something. She wiped down the coffee table with a paper towel while catching Ellie's frown that said, *Thanks for the help.*

"Mom, I don't want to go back to school. And why do I have to explain that? Why would I want to go back?"

"The old Ellie would have."

"The old Ellie didn't look like this. The old Ellie didn't have a friend die in the seat beside her. The old Ellie could walk without limping and talk without half her face looking like a monster."

Megan stopped wiping the coffee table. Mom didn't say a word.

"Maybe I'll go back if I can always walk like this, with everyone only seeing one side of me." Ellie walked close to the wall with her damaged side not visible, acting like she was meeting people. "Hello, yes, no, that's okay, I'm good over here."

Megan felt her mouth drop, and she stared wide-eyed as Ellie moved around the room.

"Why, yes, I'd love to come with you. Let me get my coat. No, no, I'll get it; you wait here." She walked away with her good side showing. "Thank you for opening the door, but I'd prefer the other side. Strange, I know, but I get carsick on that side of the car. Yes, I know that doesn't seem to make sense. The doctor calls it leftitis."

For some reason, this made Megan laugh. It was all so horrible and yet funny to imagine Ellie out in public always walking sideways.

Ellie wasn't done.

"Please, I only kiss on the cheek on first dates. And the second, and—well, okay, all of my dates . . ." Ellie continued acting. "Elspeth Anne Summerfield," she said, sounding just like the principal would at graduation. Then she walked across the room, holding a plant up by her face, pretending to take her diploma after handing the administrator the fern.

It wasn't even that funny, and yet Megan was hysterical. She couldn't stop laughing.

"Stop it!"

They turned to see Mom standing by the couch, her

knitting held against her chest. She was red in the face and shaking. Ellie and Megan froze in shock.

"Do you think it's a joke? You think you're the only one who's suffered? You don't know what it's like to get that call."

Ellie's face was pale. And Megan knew it was true—her sister had no idea the pain their parents had suffered. Ellie probably hadn't thought of what it was like for them, and even for her.

"Your dad and I went to the hospital, and they said that one of you was dead. We waited and waited to find out it was Stasia, and that you were alive. I was so happy that it was Stasia."

"Oh, Mom." Ellie crossed the room and wrapped her arms around her mother.

Mom broke down into sobs. "I was so glad."

"It's okay. I'm sorry, Mom."

Megan went to them, too, wrapping her arms around them both. They held each other for a long time, until Ellie said, "I'm sorry. This really hurts. Megan has a death grip."

They pulled away, looked at one another, and then Mom started to chuckle, and then they all laughed.

* * *

"This is my grandfather."

Ellie and Will stared at the headstone that Ellie had never seen before this evening. During the funeral, a temporary placard had rested above the open door into the ground. Now her grandfather was under there. She wondered how long it took for his body to begin decomposing. The date of his death was one week before her accident. A week before Stasia's death. If Ellie had died in the accident, her grave might be nearby, maybe right beside her grandfather's, with a headstone giving the barest facts of her entire life.

"I'm going to tell you what I would've said at my grandfather's funeral if I'd had the guts or thought it wouldn't hurt the people there."

"Okay. What would you have said?"

She walked up to the headstone and turned around. She cleared her voice. "My grandfather was a very unhappy man. I loved my grandfather. But he hated me. The more I tried to get him to love me, the more he hated me. I didn't know why. I didn't know he had a wife who broke his heart and left him because of his drinking. I didn't know that he had a lot of mental struggles, that he killed a lot of people in Vietnam, or that he was a prisoner of war for several months. I didn't know very much about my grandfather until everyone started talking about him after he died."

She paused, touching her hand to the cold granite headstone. Will stood with his arms crossed at his chest.

"This is kind of stupid, I know."

He shook his head. "Finish it."

"I guess the last thing I'd say is that I wish I'd known my grandfather when he was younger. And I hope that he finds peace."

Ellie walked back to Will. They stood side by side, staring at the headstone of Edward Blaine Summerfield III.

Will turned to her, studying her face. "That was great."

They wandered through the cemetery, looking at headstones with their dates and names. Some people had died in wars or were veterans; some couples were buried together. There was a section of people all with the same last name.

When they got back to Will's car, he said, "I could fall in love with you."

Before she could respond, he took her arms and pulled her toward him. His lips touched hers gently. He moved his fingers through her hair. "I've wanted to touch your hair for so long."

He pulled back and stared at her. With a hand on either side of her face, he touched along her jaw. She winced, but he held her face gently, with both hands. One hand on the smooth side, the other barely touching the scars.

Stepping back then, Will took a deep breath. "What would you like to do tonight?"

"Is anything happening out at Jonah's Farm?"

"Not tonight. Jonah is down in the city, I heard. We could drive to Mount Shasta for some music in the park or something."

"Sure," she said, though what she wanted was just to be with Will tonight. "Or we could go to my house."

Will shook his head. "I need to get a little more control over myself before I'm hanging out unsupervised at your house. I'm not feeling very harmless right now."

His admission sent a jolt of excitement through her. Ellie longed to go somewhere with him and escape into the feeling she had when they kissed.

As they drove to Mount Shasta, listening to an alternative band from England, they crossed Lake Shasta and its many narrow arms. It had been an unusually wet winter, she'd been told. She'd been in her bubble for so long, she'd lost all sense of seasons or awareness that weather occurred at all.

The lake had filled back up. Their footsteps on the bottom of the lake would disappear, and Ellie thought of her grandmother's bracelet buried somewhere deep underwater.

The small park in the mountain community was littered with groups of people. They got out of the car, and Will went to ask about the festivities. Ellie thought it looked like a miniature Woodstock, with some women dancing on the lawn with banners while other people smoked from bongs.

"How's it going?" a guy said, sitting on the other side of a picnic table near the car. He wore dreadlocks and a thick, woolly coat. Ellie guessed him to be in his late twenties.

"Fine." She glanced around for Will.

"Don't worry. I'm not trying to pick you up."

She self-consciously tried hiding her scarred left side.

"Not that you're not beautiful or anything. Just I saw you come here with that guy."

Ellie nodded. "Okay."

"Wanna smoke?" He wasn't holding a cigarette, but a rolled-up joint.

"It's okay. Thanks, though."

"Weed helps the pain." He motioned to her, indicating her scars. "All over the country, people smoke for medical reasons."

"Is that why you smoke it?"

"Bad back." He raised his eyebrows at that. "'Cause of my back, I get to grow my own plants. Medicinal purposes, of course."

"Of course." Ellie nodded.

Will walked up then. He greeted the guy with a nod and said, "How's it going, man?"

"Fine, really fine."

"Hey, the music is next weekend. Sorry," Will said, rubbing Ellie's arms. "But some people are getting together at a house just down the road."

"Another party?"

"A get-together."

"Of strangers?" She wanted to go home.

"Fellow music lovers."

"Potheads?"

He shrugged. "Mostly."

Ellie smiled. "You could make friends anywhere and get invited to anyone's house."

"It's my international background."

"Is that right?"

He raised an eyebrow. "So you wanna head back home, I can tell."

"I don't want to ruin your night."

"It's fine. I'm giving in to your wishes so when something's really important to me, you can't say no, no matter what."

"Sounds scary."

He laughed. "Let's get some dinner."

Partway through eating a slice of pizza, sitting in Will's car, Ellie realized with a sudden insight that she didn't like her life anymore. She looked at the cheese dripping off the end of the pizza and watched it make a slow dive down to the paper plate on her lap.

"This isn't what I'm supposed to be doing," she said.

Will looked at the string of cheese dripping down. "Most people just eat it."

"I mean, my life now and where I'm going. Or rather, not going."

Will was quiet for a few minutes, then said, "So you want things the way they were before? Your organized and driven life?"

She shook her head. "I didn't like my life then, either, though I believed that I did."

"Wow, what is this? Epiphany pizza?"

She smiled and took a bite of the cheese, eating the string of it like a long noodle. "Maybe. That guy in the park, he thought I'd like to smoke pot. To help with the pain."

"Did that bother you?"

"Not really. I think he's the first person to see my scars and just treat me normal, like my face this way is normal. And we could talk about it."

"And you don't like that, or you do?"

"Well, it caught me off guard. Plus, he's this guy I didn't know, and he was offering me weed." Ellie wondered where she'd be by that guy's age. It was the choices she made now that would determine much of it. "I need to start figuring out my life. You know, I don't like parties. It's ridiculous that I started smoking—and that's no judgment on you, and I know you tried to stop me. I just don't want to be around a bunch of people smoking pot, doing drugs, being crazy 'cause they're drinking. I want something different."

Will smiled in his usual nonchalant way. "So you're dumping me as your friend, huh?"

She laughed. "Not yet."

"Then I'll enjoy our time together. Now, eat your pizza."

* * *

Later that night, Ellie was online, reading a news report about children in Afghanistan after the war, when an IM popped up on her screen. No one ever IMed her, because she was always invisible. Of course, it was Will.

W: My real father was Brazilian.

E: Real father? Your dad isn't your real father?

W: No. My real father went to college back east
     and met my mom. His family was furious when
     he ran off and married an American. Then my
     parents divorced when I was a baby, and my
     dad returned to Brazil. A year later my mom
     married John. That's why everyone thinks John
     is my real dad, even me sometimes.

E: Interesting.

W: So when I was in fourth grade . . .

Ellie sat cross-legged on the bed and leaned closer toward the screen of her laptop.

E: Go on.

W: ☺

E: Tell me!

W: Okay, so one night aliens . . .

E: Knock it off.

W: Okay, you really want to know this?

E: Yes!

W: My mom got a call that my dad had been shot. His family said he was dying and wanted to see me before he died.

E: How was he shot?

W: Let's just say it was drug related.

E: Ohhhh.

W: Mom said no at first. But my grandparents said they'd pay for the plane ticket, that they'd take good care of me, and that it would only be for a week. And I think they promised to pay my way through college and some other stuff, I don't know, but a deal was struck.

E: But it wasn't a week.

W: No. It was nearly the entire school year—like eight months. My dad was in some kind of drug war. He was shot, and he did want to see me. But as soon as I got there, I was rushed to some safe house he was hiding in. And my grandparents had to leave me there with him and get out of there. I don't think they intended for me to stay.

E: You must have been so afraid.

W: Terrified. I had never met my dad. And then the doctor didn't show up, so I had to help with his wound every day.

E: Then they didn't want to give you back?

W: Maybe they would have, but something happened, I don't know what. We were moved somewhere new, and for a while not even my grandparents could find us. We were with a lot

of really tough people. I think I cried every
night to go home.

E: How did you get home?

W: We had to return to my grandparents' ranch after
a long time. They were so happy to find me, and
within a few days I was sent home to my mom.

E: So it's like you were kidnapped.

W: I don't think of it like that, but I guess I sort of was.

E: Wow, that's an amazing story.

W: But now I have no mystery.

E: That story is more intense and exciting than the
mystery.

W: So this new, determined Ellie. When is she coming back to school?

E: I'm not.

W: Why not?

E: Because that epiphany pizza was good, but not
that good.

W: So you aren't going to graduate with the class?

E: No.

W: What if I make you?

E: You won't. You can't.

After Ellie closed her laptop and rolled over in bed, she
thought about the many painful experiences that people
went through. She'd never have guessed that Will had gone
through all that he'd experienced. How did people move on
from such things? From heartbreak, trauma, loss, suffering,
pain, and guilt?

Beautiful

Ellie wanted her life to go somewhere. Not backward, not on the line it was currently going, but forward, somehow. But how did she do it? One step at a time, she decided. She reached for her laptop again.

E: You still there?

W: Yes.

E: What do you think of us?

W: Is this the big "us" question?

E: I just want to know what you are thinking.

W: I could play the "What are you thinking" game, but I won't. I think that . . .

E: Yes?

W: I already said it. I could fall in love with you.

Ellie felt a quick tightening through her stomach. She'd wondered a few times if that were really possible, and at times she thought she might be falling in love with Will as well. But she didn't think this was love. And as she'd wondered when she was with Ryan, *could* she even love?

W: But.

E: Oh, the big BUT.

W: I think our friendship is important and should be carefully managed. I could fall in love with you and ruin this. Because we have different paths ahead of us, we have differences that are great as friends, but I think they'd hurt us if we moved beyond that.

Ellie realized she was nodding to herself. That was exactly what she sensed. And yet, there was a strange sting of rejection attached to his logical words. Would he have said them if they'd grown this close before the accident?

W: I think I've loved you since we were kids, to be quite honest—though I shouldn't be saying this all online. But we were meant to love as friends. I know this year has been horrible, but having your friendship back is really cool. Even though you're confused and need to educate yourself in movies and books more, you are beautiful, Ellie. Now more than ever.

Chapter 20

*M*egan's graduation gown hung on a hanger in the doorway beside the new, dark blue dress she'd sewn from the same pattern as the yellow funeral dress. She was getting pretty good at sewing, she had to admit. Ellie had ironed it for her and now sat on the bed while Megan adjusted the cap on her head while looking in the mirror.

"Is there some certain way to wear it?" Megan asked in frustration.

"I don't think so. But you better put a pin in it so it doesn't fall off."

Megan looked at her sister through the reflection in the mirror. "There still might be time, you know. The administration would welcome you right on stage if you showed up."

Everyone had emphatically encouraged Ellie to graduate with her class. Her parents, family members, Vanessa, the student council, the ever-cheerful Lisa, even Megan and Will had opinions on why she shouldn't miss this night. Strangely, Ellie's counselor, Maggie, was somewhat indifferent about it, which annoyed Megan.

Ellie had relayed Maggie's words: "It's your choice. It's a milestone night, but it's not the most important, not even close. You have been making progress in your life. This night could make that better or worse. But you have to be the one to decide."

But Megan both agreed and disagreed. She understood how hard it'd be for Ellie to be the subject of hundreds, maybe thousands of people's interest. And it was only one night, something that life didn't hinge upon. But Megan also remembered Ellie making plans with Vanessa to wear bright, matching shoes to graduation, and her sister had helped with the graduation and Sober Grad Night in the previous years at school. Now she wouldn't be there for her own. She'd missed prom, senior portraits, class rings, graduation invitations, senior trips and banquets, and this was the final thing she'd miss before it was over. Megan thought she might regret it.

"I can't. I don't want to. But I'm sorry that I'm not going to watch you." Ellie's voice wavered as she said it.

Megan laughed. "Like I told you, I don't care."

"You have to care. It's graduation."

"It really doesn't matter that much to me. You never believe me on these things. It really isn't that big of a deal to me. It was to you."

"Yeah. It *was*."

"You would've given a speech."

Ellie nodded and adjusted herself on the bed. "Yes, everyone would've loved for the burned freak to inspire them all. I could have talked about overcoming obstacles, about how this was the best thing that ever happened to me, how God was good through it all. They might have cried and said things about it being the best speech they'd ever heard and how tragic it was for someone like me to have this happen to her, but how amazing that I'd risen above the tragedy to find the good in it."

Sometimes Megan felt impatient with her sister's self-pity. Sure, if anyone deserved to wallow in it, it was Ellie. But it grew tiring. "You'll always be a 'burned freak' until you decide not to be."

"Whatever. That's easy for you to say."

Megan stood with her hands on her hips. "No, actually, it isn't easy at all."

They were both silent for a while. Ellie rolled up the cord to the iron.

Megan sighed and sat on the edge of the bed. She seriously hated these heart-to-heart conversations, but Ellie needed to hear this. "El, this was your graduation, even more than mine. I'm not disappointed that you won't be there. If you'll regret it years from now, I wish you'd attend it, for you. If you won't regret it, then I'm glad you don't have to face an incredibly painful night. Only you will feel the pain of it; everyone else will be happy and oblivious to your pain and trying to ignore their own fear. You are the face that reminds them of mortality and that the very best of people will go through the very worst of life."

Ellie smiled at that.

Megan was confused. She thought that would offend her sister. "Why are you smiling?"

"Only you would state the most blatant and painful truths."

"We both know it; we might as well admit it. The thing is, I know you'll be okay. You really will be better than ever. Everything in the speech you could have made, it'll all be true. I don't really doubt that."

"Well, I guess one good thing that came out of this is that I have my very rude and obnoxious sister back in my life."

Megan smiled. "God works in mysterious ways."

* * *

The house vibrated with emptiness, like a thousand drops of water on a pond with ripples rolling throughout the rooms.

They'd been gone for an hour, rushing out with gown and balloons and gifts. Dad gave a final look her way before closing the door, an expression that asked, *Are you sure?*

Ellie watched TV, then turned on the bathwater. Then suddenly she turned off the tap and searched for her shoes. She picked up her dad's car keys and grabbed her coat—the one with the hood that she'd hated in the past.

It was late May, and some people would be there in shorts and tank tops. She was wearing jeans and a T-shirt with a small Peter Pan in the center. It was an outfit that Ryan would've loved. She'd always found it amusing that he liked her dressed simply even better than all dressed up.

Cars lined both sides of the road leading into the school. The parking lots were probably full. She drove along anyway, coming closer to the football field, where the giant lights blazed upon the grounds. A couple jogged toward the entrance, and also a family. The man swept up his little girl to hurry them all along.

She couldn't find an open spot. But through the fence she could see the maroon gowns of the graduates moving across the field. She pulled along the curb near the fence, somewhat blocking traffic, but no cars were moving now. Everyone was inside or hurrying there on foot. On the other side of the chain-link fence, her friends since childhood and her sister were walking amidst a growing cheer from the audience that could be heard even with her windows rolled up.

She could still make it. She could run inside and wave as they walked in. She could be there when their class was announced and be swept into the hugs and cheers and photographs.

The first words were just out of hearing, even as she rolled down her window. She could make out a few things here and there. Still no cars came down that parking lot row, so she finally pushed open the car door and walked to the fence. Through the fence she could see the football field showered in light, while she was in relative darkness. She held the cold metal fence and strained to see the graduates, who were all in their seats now, but it was too far. There was some cheering, and a girl made her way to the podium.

Melissa Lopez was salutatorian. She spoke about leaving their high school years, going forward into a new future, but always cherishing what they'd had together at West Redding High. Then came Bly, who gave the valedictorian speech. He made everyone laugh. Then it was time for the class president's speech. Ellie waited for Carrie Lincoln, the class vice president, to be called in her place. Instead, Ellie's name was called.

"Elspeth Summerfield could not be with us tonight to accept this award of excellence, and so her sister, Megan Summerfield, will accept it in her honor."

Ellie could see her sister walking up to the stage. Mom was probably crying, and maybe a few others in her class as well.

Megan cleared her throat. "I wish my sister could be with us tonight. It's been a very difficult year for our family. But it has also drawn us closer. My sister had done a lot of great things in her life. It's great that she was recognized like this. I'm proud of her, and she's the strongest, most beautiful human being that I've ever met. I accept this for her. Thank you."

Ellie felt the tears on her face before she knew she was crying. The applause rose and continued rising. People were standing, rising from the bleachers, and her class stood as well. Ellie leaned her forehead against the fence and closed her eyes.

The school superintendent came to the podium. "Tonight is a night of celebration and accomplishment. For a moment, however, we'd like to remember Stasia Fuller. A moment of silence, please."

The moment was simply that, a pause in the program, and then Stasia was once again forgotten, just as Ellie was. The night was for those who were there, not for those left behind.

The names began, with cheers and applause from the crowd growing as they went down the list.

Ryan Blasing

Vanessa Hart

William Stefanos

Megan Marie Summerfield

And all the other names she knew, many since they were in kindergarten and grammar school together. They'd walked in the town parade, played catch-and-kiss, acted in school plays, teased each other for missing front teeth, and watched as they grew from children to adults.

"Please stand with me to congratulate the graduating class . . ." And the hats flew into the air like fireworks with the sound of cheering, whistles, and applause.

Ellie wished to capture them there, to hold the caps up in the air, freezing time, going back in time, or just resting for a while as the world waited.

The world didn't wait.

She was so behind everything, when before, she was always ahead, always full out in front of everyone else and right on the hem of tomorrow.

Ellie drove home before anyone would know that she'd been out. The house was exactly the same as when she'd left an hour earlier. She just wanted to crawl into bed and either sleep or cry.

Megan wouldn't come home tonight—she was attending Sober Grad Night, which seemed an oxymoron. Will was leaving in the morning for his trip to Brazil for his cousin's wedding.

Ellie heard her parents' arrival. It didn't sound as if her aunts or anyone else had come with them. She hoped they'd leave her alone. She didn't want to hear about the ceremony or act as if she hadn't been there. She didn't want them to give her the award or be told that she'd received a standing ovation.

Someone tapped on her bedroom door. She ignored it, but Mom peeked her head in anyway. "Someone's here to see you."

"What?" Ellie sat up, surprised. "Who?"

But Mom had already disappeared, leaving the door open a crack. Ellie went to the hall and listened to the voices coming from the living room. She had to walk closer and closer to the stairwell before she recognized the voice talking with her parents.

"Hi," she said, walking into the living room.

"Hi," Ryan said.

There was an awkward silence, and then her parents left, offering final congratulations to Ryan.

"Yeah, congratulations," Ellie said to him.

"Thanks. And congrats to you," he said with a wide grin that made her heart literally skip a beat.

"I haven't actually graduated yet. I think it's official in a few weeks."

"Then congrats early. You look good, really good. I like the haircut too," he said with that old, admiring look in his eye.

She wanted to give a flippant response, something that stated the obvious, reminding him of her disfigured face. She realized she was in the jeans and Peter Pan shirt that she'd earlier thought he would have loved.

"You look great too." He was more the Ryan she'd known before, and also older and stronger.

"I went through a bad stint, but I've come through it. And now I'm a graduate." He stood taller, acting as if he was proud, which made her laugh.

"So, are you going to Sober Grad Night?" Ellie asked.

"Yeah. I have an extra ticket, if you want to go."

She smiled and shook her head. "No, but thanks. Why do you have an extra ticket?"

"Just got one, just in case."

"What about Tara?"

"I never wanted to go out with Tara. But after you didn't

want me, I guess it was flattering for a brief time. I found her boring." He laughed at that. "So I have this extra Sober Grad ticket for you."

"That was nice. Thanks, but, you know. Your parents aren't throwing you a graduation party?"

"Actually, they are. I gotta get over there pretty quick. My family from the Bay Area is all up. I'm going to school down there next year."

"Really?" she said and felt a sting of both pride and sadness. Pride that he was getting out of Redding—something she had wondered if he'd do. And sadness at his leaving and that she knew so little about his life now.

"You had a lot to do with that."

She shook her head. "No. You did that."

"But I might not have without being with someone so full of dreams." He glanced down a moment, then picked up a small gift from the coffee table. He handed it to her. "I brought you a graduation gift."

Ryan still surprised her with the unexpected. "Do I have to wait till I have my diploma before I open it?"

"It can be a pre-gift." He sat on the couch then, and Ellie followed. "Usually I'd exit now. It's weird being in the room when someone opens your gift, I think. But I want to see your face with this one."

Guessing that it was jewelry, her self-consciousness grew. But she was pleased as well at the thought. "Your mom wrapped it, huh?"

He shook his head and laughed. "You have no faith in me. I did it all myself."

"I am impressed." And she was. The little gold wrapping

with the bow was so perfect, she hesitated to open it. Inside was a small white box. Ellie lifted the lid, then opened the folded tissue paper.

She saw gold, then the weaving of gold.

A bracelet.

It looked exactly like her grandmother's.

"Where did you get this? It looks just like mine."

"It is yours." He nodded proudly.

It was nearly too unreal to believe. "How?" was all that came out. Then, "But I thought . . . When did you find it?"

"A few weeks after the accident. Or maybe a month. I don't know. You were still in ICU down at Davis. I could only get in to see you a few times, and my parents made me come home. So I'd go out to the lake every day after school. My dad borrowed those metal detectors. But we couldn't find it. Then it started to rain. I actually prayed. And that day I saw something shining—maybe the rain loosened some dirt or helped it catch the light just right."

Ellie shook her head in disbelief as Ryan took the bracelet out of the box. He gently took her arm and put the bracelet around her wrist. The touch of his fingers sent shivers through her arm.

"I can't even begin to thank you for this, Ryan. It's incredible."

He smiled triumphantly. "I nearly gave it to you a few times. But then we broke up and everything. I decided I'd mail it to you, or drop it off in a box on your doorstep. Then I decided to give it to you for a graduation gift."

Ellie didn't know what to say. "I'm so sorry. I'm so sorry for everything."

"Me too, Els." He gave her a hug then, pulling her against his chest.

She smelled his cologne—the same scent she'd loved for so long.

"You know I'll always love you. I'm going away to school for a while. And you have things you need to do in your life. But maybe, I'm hoping . . . maybe if and when it's right, you'll fall madly in love with me too. Hopefully I'll still be available," he teased.

A flood of emotion filled her. "I do love you, you know. Thank you for that. And thank you for this." There was such a lightness within her. "And yes, maybe, if . . ."

"*Maybe* could keep the world going around," he said with that smile of his and a raised eyebrow. "I better get going now. There's a little note at the bottom of the box as well. I'm not sticking around to watch you read that."

"Keep in touch, okay?"

He wrapped his arms around her for another long hug that she wished would never end. "Oh, you betcha. You can't get rid of me so easily, Els. I'll be over to bug you over the summer. And next year I'll be on the webcam, asking for homework help."

She laughed.

At the door, he turned back. "You sure you don't want to just stop by Sober Grad?"

Her heart raced with panic at the idea. She bit her lip and thought of the text messages she'd received that night from a large number of her friends, telling her they missed her.

Ryan noticed her hesitation. "You could text Vanessa and

a few of your friends, so it won't be this huge surprise. And I'll take you home as soon as you want."

Ellie knew she was so close to being past this. After tonight, the pressure would be gone to go back to school, to go to graduation. But what if she should do this? She'd missed graduation, and that couldn't come back.

"Okay, then."

* * *

Megan was waiting with Vanessa and the guys near the entrance to the country club that hosted Sober Grad. A balloon arch covered the entrance, and CONGRATULATIONS, GRADUATES! hung above the balloons.

Ryan walked one protective step ahead of her. And then Ellie was pulled into a swarm. Vanessa was crying, and Ellie started crying too.

"I'm so glad you came. I've missed you terribly."

Everyone was hugging her, crying and saying how they missed her, how sorry they were for everything she'd gone through. Over the loudspeaker someone announced, "Our graduation is complete. Ellie Summerfield has entered the building, folks. Welcome, Ellie. This wouldn't be the same without you."

Ellie was surprised at the welcome, and equally surprised at her lack of self-consciousness. Perhaps Maggie would call this progress, but all Ellie knew was that she felt a sudden sense of belonging. Everyone was happy; they were saying good-bye even as they said hello, because this was their class's final night together. They talked about their years together, about crushes and field trips. A few times someone would see her and the shock was apparent on his or her face. But that surprise would quickly dissolve into exuberance. They really did love her. And Ellie found the sudden rekindled love for her childhood friends.

While sitting with Megan, Vanessa, Ryan, and a number of their other friends around the swimming pool, a girl with a giant roll of raffle tickets stopped in front of Ellie. "I've wanted to talk to you for so long."

It was Lisa, the organizer of Ellie's fan club. She had volunteered for Sober Grad just as Ellie had done in years past.

"I've been a bit reclusive."

"I understand. It's okay. Just know that I'm here, even with school out." The girl appeared nervous in Ellie's actual presence.

Ellie thanked her. When Lisa said good-bye, holding up her raffle tickets to prove she had somewhere to go, Ellie called her back.

"Yes?" Lisa asked with a youthful earnestness.

"Have fun while you do all this. And don't make all this stuff your life. Remember to have your own life too."

Lisa looked confused but said she would, and hurried away.

Ellie was growing tired. She called Dad to pick her up, not wanting Ryan to leave the party. Once a student left Sober Grad, he couldn't return—part of the rules toward keeping it sober.

"Are you glad you came?" Megan asked, sitting beside her and lacing her arm through Ellie's. That was something her sister had never done before.

Ellie nodded. "Are you? I never expected you for a school function, rebel that you are."

"Yeah, shocking, isn't it? And what's more shocking, it's been great."

"I guess it's a new beginning for both of us."

"Yes, it is, little sister. A new beginning."

Chapter 21

THE OUTSIDER

The No-Longer-Anonymous Blog about Life at West
  Redding High

June 6

Farewell, friends. To new beginnings!

* * *

Y ou poor neglected baby," Ellie said to her green Karmann
  Ghia, running her hand over the smooth slope of the
hood. It had sat under the carport through the long winter.

Dad had taken her car to the auto shop while she was in
the hospital. They had fixed the alternator and given it a
tune-up. When she'd told him her plan for the day, he pulled
out the car and checked the fluids and the tires. He understood her need to go somewhere, to go to the ocean alone.

The engine started right up.

"Stay overnight if you get tired," Mom said, wringing a dish
towel with her hands. "Don't forget your hat and sunscreen."

Of course Mom didn't want Ellie to go, and Ellie wished
she didn't have to add to her mother's worry and anxiety.
Mom had experienced enough of that in the past six months.
But Ellie wanted this as she hadn't wanted anything in years.

Maybe not since she was a little girl wishing for that Easy-Bake Oven so she could cook delightful treats for her family. The desire to sit by the sea and fill her lungs with salt air was nearly overpowering.

Ellie put the car into first gear, and it moved forward down the driveway. The steering wheel felt loose and the brake too touchy. She was happy to get down the street and beyond the concern of her parents. By the time she crested the rise out of Redding to the view of the blue waters of Whiskeytown Lake, it was as if the car knew where to go. And with every mile, Ellie felt stronger, freer, and more excited about her first little trip alone. Even though her left side was exposed to the outside world, to cars passing her and the wind from the cracked window moving her hair off her burns, she didn't care about any of it.

The two-and-a-half-hour drive from Redding to the coast was a winding cruise over the mountains and down to the sea. The blue sky met with a blanket of fog as she went through the final range to the sand dunes outside of Arcata.

Ellie missed Megan, but her sister was checking out a college with one of her friends in southern Oregon anyway. Will was in Brazil, and though she missed him and he'd written how he wished she could've come, Ellie was glad they'd remained in "friends only" territory. Ryan might have been fun to bring on this mini road trip, but this drive was something she needed to do alone.

She turned north and wished she could just drive and drive, up the rocky northern coastline of California to Oregon and Washington. For now, she would settle for the little coastal hamlet of Harper's Bay.

The directions her dad had given her were easy enough. She pulled into the sandy parking lot beside a number of other vehicles. It wasn't even noon yet. She had the whole day to herself.

For a moment, an awkward feeling came over her that nearly kept her inside. She'd never done something like this alone. It would be intimidating even without her face the way it was.

I can go to the beach by myself.

Pushing her door open, she hopped out quickly before she thought more about it. Mom had packed a small ice chest. Ellie grabbed her beach bag and dropped an ice-cold water inside. Throwing a thin wrap around her shoulders and plopping the wide-brimmed hat over her head, she guessed she appeared older, but she had to protect her scars from the sun. Next she tossed off her shoes and slipped on flip-flops, then locked her car and headed for the sandy rise between the beach and the parking lot. A breeze blew lightly against her face, and the sand was thick and deep as she walked.

At the top of the rise, she paused, taking in the view. A gray-blue wave came rolling up and then slid against the sand. The fog had cleared, and the sky was a vivid blue. There was a straight line on the horizon where sea and sky met. Giant black rocks rose from the sand along the beach, and Ellie remembered that many had shallow caves and tunnels to explore when the tide was low.

She walked close to the water, and waves came rising up to circle her feet and ankles, then made a gentle coaxing tug back toward the sea.

After a while, her left leg started throbbing from the walk. She climbed up a porous black rock to a ledge that stretched over the water about halfway up. The climb was a bit precarious, but she made it and sat down with a feeling of accomplishment.

While snacking on a pack of pistachios, Ellie watched two teenage girls run down to the water. They wore bikini tops and shorts and laughed at how cold the water was on their legs. Their boyfriends—Ellie presumed them to be boyfriends—quickly joined them, one with a wet suit and a surfboard.

Their skin was tanned, and they ran and splashed with utter freedom. One girl did a spontaneous dive into a wave and came up laughing, her hair wet from the sea. And Ellie knew these girls could have been her a year ago. That could be her kicking up wet sand behind her feet as she ran toward the waves. That was her, comfortable in a bikini and in skin she didn't even think to be grateful for, not a care in the world.

And what did she look like now? To them, unless they came close, Ellie could be an old woman. A woman with a wide-brimmed hat and long sleeves, dark Jackie O glasses, skin wrinkled on one side of her face. An old woman sitting by the sea, watching as if decades had passed since she'd been one of those girls.

All the pain and suffering of the world attached itself to her like a thousand leeches that sucked the blood and life from her veins. What could she do with all the pain?

She knew suffering now. She knew pain. They were closer companions than all her friends had been for her entire life.

Ellie thought again of the note Ryan had put in the bottom of the bracelet box. She'd read it over and over.

You know what I figured out through all this, Els? Everybody is disfigured in some way or another. Some people are worse than others. In some people, we see it immediately in their faces or bodies. But everyone has broken places. Just like everyone has beautiful places. You'll use your scars and your beauty for the purpose God made you for. I look forward to seeing that.

She would never look the way she used to. But in a year, maybe two, and the years after, her scars would be less and less evident. Guys might check her out on the street, instead of children crying out in horror. But Ryan was right. Everyone was disfigured in one way or another.

With every wave, the footprints of the couples on the beach disappeared. Ellie's footprints had already been smoothed from the sand. Long ago, her family had come here on vacation. They had run along this beach, and the water picked up the memory of them and took it out to sea.

Ellie had an idea. She picked up her stuff and made the trek back toward the parking lot. After rummaging through her car, she nearly gave up. Then she spotted a small store at the dock. She walked, with her jeans still rolled up, across the parking lot, passing a store window with seashells and wind chimes visible from the window. The scent of sea and fish grew stronger, and boats creaked on their mooring lines in the small harbor.

The clerk watched her with that look of interest and sympathy that she often saw on faces when people saw her scars. But it didn't bother her much now, and she brushed it away and acted as if she didn't notice.

The scent of fresh-baked sourdough bread drew her inside a small diner, where she ate a bread bowl filled with hot clam chowder. She drank cold Perrier and dropped little oyster crackers into the soup. *So this is what it's like to be independent, strong, and out in the world,* she thought, smiling to herself.

Back at her car, Ellie found a piece of paper and pen. She tried several ideas as she watched a kite whipping in the air above the beach.

Ellie wouldn't become like her grandfather, though she could. The bitterness would destroy her if she let it. She had blamed God, though now she felt that she knew Him more. Growing slowly within her was a deep longing and wonder toward the mystery of God.

There was much she could write on the paper. Something about the accident, about Stasia, about the people she'd loved and lost and those she had recently gained. But in the end, Ellie wrote one word, then rolled up the paper and slid it into the empty Perrier bottle. She screwed on the lid and headed back to the water.

She could be so many things, so many people. So much life stretched ahead of her, with countless possibilities. With a sea before her and a million options to choose from, Ellie gently tossed the bottle out into the water.

Her grandfather had said she'd never amount to anything. He was wrong. All her work had been to be someone of value and importance, and that had been wrong as well. Now she was scarred and changed. She was herself, and that was worth everything.

Chapter 22

THE OUTSIDER
College Edition
October 17

As I'm now living with relatives just across the bridge from San Francisco, I felt that qualified the continued title for my blog of "The Outsider." So this will be the college edition, as I will be taking the BART into the city where I'm attending community college. If you're looking for movie, music, and restaurant reviews, this is the place to check out. It's also musings about purpose, faith, and God. Yes, I'm growing up, and you have to read about it if you want to enjoy those other things. I won't lose my sarcastic tone, don't worry. God made me that way. I still think people are stupid.

* * *

Megan sat at the outdoor café with her hand wrapped around a large cappuccino. A cable car rang its bell and stopped on the rails in the center of the street. People hopped on and off—businesspeople and tourists alike—then the red car made a dip down one of San Francisco's infamously hilly streets.

"I better get going," Jasmine said, picking up her large bag. "See you in class tomorrow."

"Okay," Megan said to her lone friend in the city. They'd met in class and had quickly become friends—a rare thing for Megan. "And don't forget to pick up the tickets for Friday."

Jasmine smiled her usual wide grin that looked stunning against her deep bronze skin. "You got it."

Megan remained at the table, laptop open in front of her, realizing this was the first time she'd sat at a café alone. Her transition from Redding to city life hadn't been easy. Aunt Betty was driving her crazy, but she provided a free room with an outdoor entrance. Especially in the first month, Megan missed home. She missed her parents, even. But mostly she missed her sister. It annoyed her that homesickness had threatened to send her back, but after a couple of months in college, she was finally settling in and feeling more comfortable.

And besides, Ellie wasn't home either.

"Can I get you anything else?" the waitress asked.

"Are you taking applications?" Megan asked.

The woman laughed. "Not at the moment. What kind of job are you looking for?"

"Any job that pays," Megan said.

The woman picked up some menus from another table. "What experience do you have?"

Megan figured she'd be honest. "I could bring in my meager résumé."

"Have you done any writing?"

Megan smiled. "A little. A blog, like the rest of the world."

"Bring in some samples. I own this place and a little

online news site—local reviews and news. The guy who worked with me on it moved to New York. You'd be like a local critic."

Megan couldn't believe her casual job query could open up such an opportunity. "I'll bring you some samples later today."

"Great," the woman said. "I kind of have a feeling about you, though. Get online and check out the site too."

Megan decided to do it then and there as the woman went to get her another cappuccino. Reading through a few articles and reviews, Megan knew her style would fit perfectly. She'd never have guessed her tone and attitude might become a commodity.

Then she noticed the date on the computer. It had been one year today.

A year ago, their lives were completely different. Ellie was getting ready for a date with Ryan, and Megan couldn't stand her sister.

She closed her laptop, sliding it back into her satchel before heading for the bus.

A paid critic—who could have guessed it? It was perfect for her.

* * *

The traffic pressed around from all sides, and it appeared that no one in the entire country of Peru observed any laws of the road. At an intersection, they waited at a red light with numerous vehicles—carts, motorcycles, scooters, and bicyclists on rickety bikes—surrounding the van up to its windows and doors.

Ellie sat in the front passenger seat, pushed against the glass with a little girl stretched out asleep between her and the driver, Raymond. The girl's curly black hair covered Ellie's lap.

They were all tired, and most everyone in the van was asleep—her four team members and the ten children who were moving to their new home.

Outside the window, Ellie saw the passing vehicles go through the intersection: a young Peruvian man listening to an iPod, with several pigs in the back of his truck; an old woman hunched close to the steering wheel in a rusty car; some rich-looking guys in a new Mercedes; a small child of about eight on a large bicycle, standing off the seat and pumping hard on the pedals as he tried to keep up with the Mercedes.

Each of the passing individuals was lost within his or her own world. They had destinations in mind, friends and families, hopes and dreams.

The sound of a Spanish guitarist suddenly erupted from her purse, making Raymond glance her way.

"You keep your eyes on the road," Ellie teased as he headed into the chaos of the intersection. She dug around in her purse, careful not to wake the little girl.

She'd set all her ringtones to Spanish music several months ago, before she left for Peru. This international text was from Ryan. He'd insisted on paying for the added service to their phones while she was gone.

Ryan: How's Super Els?

She smiled at his new name for her and texted back:

It was a hard but good day.
Ryan: Did you get the kids?

Ellie glanced back to the rows of children and noticed one little boy staring out the window. Everyone else was asleep.

Ellie: We did.
Ryan: That's another progressive step in changing
     the world.
Ellie: A slow progression.

The little girl shifted in her seat as Raymond hit the brakes and then lurched forward again. How he missed hitting people and vehicles, she had no idea.

Ellie: The conditions were terrible.

They had bathed the children at a local church before heading out of the city. It might have been the first bath they'd had in months, or even longer. They'd picked up the kids from a temporary housing unit. The people there couldn't feed the kids any longer and were sending them out to the streets in a matter of days.

Gangs of children survived in the back alleys of countless cities throughout South America. The aid organization Ellie was with was building orphanages, schools, and free clinics. It was slow progress, the director told her, but every life was precious.

The girl had stared at Ellie, as the children often did. They stared at her face and came to a conclusion.

"*Cómo se llama?*" Ellie asked.

"*Esperanza,*" the child said and crawled into Ellie's lap.

"Her name means 'hope,'" Raymond said.

Ellie nodded. She almost said, *Of course.* Ellie thought of Pandora's box—or jar, as Will would correct—and how hope was saved from being lost among the evils of the world. Maybe she'd write to Will that she'd found *Hope* in more than one way since she'd come here.

Ryan: Are you okay?
Ellie: Yes. I really am.
Ryan: I know you already know what today is.
Ellie: Yes.

It had been exactly one year. Only one year that felt like decades. A year ago, Ryan had surprised her with a candlelit path to a sunset picnic. Grandfather's funeral was over, by only a day.

A year ago, Ellie's house was still full of relatives, she'd lost the bracelet that was now on her wrist, Megan had worn the yellow dress and still hated her, and Ellie had talked to Will for the first time in years outside on the back patio. This was the date they'd gone to Mitch's house. It was the day Stasia left the earth, and Ellie stayed behind with scars to testify to her survival.

Ellie: The day my life changed.

She was in Peru for another month. Then she'd start college in the spring semester, though she wasn't sure which school she'd be attending. Ellie wasn't sure about anything in the future, which was both scary and exciting.

She thought of the bottle she'd tossed into the ocean several months earlier on her first trip alone. Where was that bottle now? she wondered. Could it have made its way along some ocean current to the South American coast, as she had? Or had someone found it by now? Ellie would never know. She hadn't included her address or phone number. And there was only one word on the paper.

Ellie.

It was a one-word declaration that said it all. For that was who she was. And that was who she would be. And God would complete the work He had begun in her, and her life did and would matter. And she knew that she was no longer afraid to love.

They were barely out of the city when Raymond slowed for a herd of sheep that were crossing the road.

Ellie: Sheep parade again.

Then she looked back at the little boy staring out the window. He was smiling and waving at the sheep. He saw her looking at him, and he smiled at her as well.

The children loved her, because she knew them without ever having met them. She was one of them, a survivor of pain. They saw her, touched the scars that would never fully disappear. They needed no words of explanation.

"You have a gift, you know," Raymond had told Ellie.

Ryan: Gotta get to my last class. Know that you're
    loved in the North.
Ellie: And you in the South.

She slid her phone into her bag and watched the sun falling toward the sharp peaks of the Andes.

Touching a curl in Esperanza's hair, Ellie took in a deep breath and wondered about all that waited ahead. It was more than she could imagine, and that seemed exactly how it should be.

Acknowledgments

Natalie Hanemann—my wonderful editor with a golden heart! You provided essential guidance with this manuscript that created a much richer story. I can't thank you enough for that, and I appreciate your love of words and story while always caring deeply for the readers. It's a blessing working with you.

LB Norton—it should be wrong to have this much fun doing the line edits with an editor, but you make it a joy. And the book simply shines with your touch.

The Thomas Nelson fiction team—it's a blessing to be part of such a wonderful group. Thank you!

Janet Kobobel Grant—dear agent and friend, thank you as always always always.

Nieldon Coloma—thank you for your beautiful love that surrounds and uplifts me. You've brought healing to my soul and excitement for our new horizons. You are a gift from God.

Madelyn, Cody, and Weston Martinusen—you each never cease to inspire and amaze me. I'm honored to have such unique and wonderful people as my children. Your mom loves you, this much and more!

Amanda Darrah—my beautiful Aloha sister, how I miss you and treasure all that you bring to my life, and I always will. It's only the beginning.

Jenna Benton—your daily morning prayers and Jenna

stories carried me through challenging times, thank you friend (Sylvia!). You mean so much to me, Jenna Jane.

Kimberly Carlson—my sister-friend who understands this love of words perfectly. I hold you in my heart, my wolf-woman friend.

Kate Martinusen—sister-friend since 3rd grade and forever more. I love who you are and can't wait to see the next journey God is taking you on.

Alanna Ramsey—what an amazing journey of friendship we've been on. You are always loved, and I still owe you a night out eating hot dogs (even if I only eat them once a year).

Mom—You provide such support, laughter, and love that grows and grows. I appreciate and admire you beyond words. And I love you too!

Dad—I've loved the extra time we've had together in the past few years. I'll treasure it always. Thanks for the many days you made my lunch and all the fun stories you shared.

And to my little sister Jennifer Harman—sometimes called "the good sister"—though this story doesn't mirror our own, we sure had our childhood days of fighting. I'm glad you grew out of that, just kidding. :) We've been there for each other through such painful times but also the most wonderful of times. No one makes me laugh like you—and at the weirdest of things. I'm so blessed to have you as both beloved sister and friend. Onward toward many more adventures in the future—go McCormick sisters! I love you Jenny.

Finally, to you, the reader. I hope you embrace the beauty created within you, and that you discover more and more the beauty of God Himself.

Reading Group Guide

1. Which sister did you identify with the most—Megan or Ellie? In what ways did the journey of the sisters' lives influence your life?

2. Do you have a sister or a best friend that is like a sister? How has that sister-relationship helped you? How has it been hard and brought feelings of insecurity and/or jealousy? Are their ways you can improve your sister-relationships, feel more secure about yourself and more okay about your differences?

3. In what ways has your self-image hindered you from seeking your dreams?

4. What are some of the most beautiful aspects of your friends and family members? What are the most beautiful aspects of you?

5. Have you experienced a tragedy that made you feel like no one could understand or relate? Where can you go for help and healing?

6. What are your thoughts and struggles with the idea that every person is beautiful?

7. What do you find meaningful?

8. What makes you feel beautiful? What doesn't make you feel beautiful? Are there ways for you to come to peace with your self-image and believe that your worth and value are not attached to physical attributes?

9. Do you believe that God loves some people more than

others? How do you think God views you? Do you think God created beauty in every person? In what ways can you become closer to God and see more of the beauty he created within you?

10. What do you think are some of the purposes in life? How can you be beautiful in those purposes?